He'd dre␣␣␣␣␣␣␣␣ for fi␣␣␣␣␣␣␣␣

T. J. Cauthen had counted the months, the days, the hours…the heartbeats it took to survive from one minute to the next. And he'd lived through *this* moment more times than he could remember, imagining the warm sunshine on his face and the exhilaration of freedom pounding through his veins.

"You need a lift, son?" An elderly man lounged against the front fender of a battered Taurus station wagon with Fred's Taxi And Delivery Service emblazoned on the front door. He gave T.J. a slow head-to-toe survey. "I don't think I've seen you in these parts before."

"Nope."

"Know where you're goin'?"

T.J. knew exactly where he was going. He had to figure out who'd set him up. So he had to find Abby Hilliard. He'd done an Internet search for her address, clicked on the "show me a map" button and printed off the map of this entire town with a star indicating the location of her house.

Because whether she knew it or not, Abby was going to help him clear his name.

Dear Reader,

A man betrayed...who has lost his family, career and five years of his life while incarcerated for a crime he didn't commit. How far will he go to clear his name?

A widow...who endured a difficult marriage and is now determined to build an independent and successful life of her own. What will she risk to help a man whose darkest secrets could threaten her future?

And a child...who has lost everyone she has ever loved, but has a chance at new beginnings, if she can just open her heart.

The healing power of love and the forging of family bonds are powerful themes in romance. I hope you'll enjoy this story of three people who truly deserve a happy ending!

I love hearing from readers and promise to write back. I can send you newsletters or other free promotional items if you send a SASE to P.O. Box 2550, Cedar Rapids, Iowa, 52406-2550. Also, please stop by my Web site for contests, a free cookbook and information on upcoming releases.

Wishing you all the best in 2004,

Roxanne Rustand

www.roxannerustand.com
www.booksbyrustand.com

Operation: Second Chance
Roxanne Rustand

TORONTO • NEW YORK • LONDON
AMSTERDAM • PARIS • SYDNEY • HAMBURG
STOCKHOLM • ATHENS • TOKYO • MILAN • MADRID
PRAGUE • WARSAW • BUDAPEST • AUCKLAND

ISBN 0-373-71185-9

OPERATION: SECOND CHANCE

This edition published by arrangement with Harlequin Books S.A.

® and TM are trademarks of the publisher. Trademarks indicated with
® are registered in the United States Patent and Trademark Office, the
Canadian Trade Marks Office and in other countries.

Visit us at www.eHarlequin.com

Printed in U.S.A.

Acknowledgments

Many thanks to Diane Palmer, Jeanne P. Adams, Sue Crouse
and attorney Mary Strand for their invaluable assistance
with the research for this book.

Dedication

With love to my mom, Arline, and to Larry, Andy, Brian
and Emily, who always encouraged my dreams.

Books by Roxanne Rustand

HARLEQUIN SUPERROMANCE

857—HER SISTER'S CHILDREN
895—MONTANA LEGACY
946—THE HOUSE AT BRIAR LAKE
982—RODEO!
1008—A MONTANA FAMILY
1064—OPERATION: KATIE
1096—OPERATION: MISTLETOE
1165—CHRISTMAS AT SHADOW CREEK

Don't miss any of our special offers. Write to us at the
following address for information on our newest releases.

Harlequin Reader Service
U.S.: 3010 Walden Ave., P.O. Box 1325, Buffalo, NY 14269
Canadian: P.O. Box 609, Fort Erie, Ont. L2A 5X3

CHAPTER ONE

HE'D DREAMED of this day for five long years. Counted the months, the days, the hours…the heartbeats it took to survive from one minute to the next. And he'd lived through this moment times beyond measure, imagining the warm sunshine on his face and the exhilaration of freedom pounding through his veins.

But now, standing at the bus stop in Silver Springs, Wyoming, with a cheap duffel bag in one hand and a yellowed envelope in the other, T. J. Cauthen felt so isolated, so bereft, that he might have climbed back on that Greyhound if it hadn't already left in a loud rumble of exhaust.

"You need a lift, son?" An elderly man sporting a Yankees cap and rainbow suspenders lounged against the fender of a battered Taurus station wagon with Fred's Taxi and Delivery Service emblazoned on the front door. He gave T.J. a slow, head-to-toe survey. "I don't think I've seen you in these parts before."

"Nope."

"Know where you're goin'?"

"Yeah."

He knew exactly where to go because he'd done an Internet search for Abby Hilliard's address, clicked on the "show me a map" button, and printed off the map of her entire town with a star indicating the location of her house.

And he knew exactly what she looked like, too. The newspaper clipping in the envelope in his hand, from a country-club fund-raiser in 1999, showed a young woman with an upswept hairdo and diamonds glittering at her throat, on the arm of her late husband, Oren. Her cold smile and bored expression told him all he needed to know about the kind of woman she was.

The old man lingered, his eyes behind his bi-focals alive with curiosity.

"Got relatives here?"

"Nope." Certainly an astute question, and one that slipped into dangerous territory.

Who, after all, would land in this town if they didn't have kin drawing them back? The bus had passed the length of Main Street before stopping in front of Al's Beer and Burger. From what T.J. could see, Silver Springs was a dying town, with grand old homes slipping into genteel poverty along the main drag and a tumble of shabby houses along the perimeter. The kind of town most teenagers dreamed of leaving.

Giving the guy a friendly, noncommittal grin, T.J. slung the duffel over one shoulder and started walking. Without turning back, he knew that the man was watching him, every step of the way.

So he kept going. Past his turn on Lark. Past Birch and Hawthorne and Poplar, before he finally turned left down Boulder, strolled a few blocks and then doubled back on Oak. His habit of caution came back to him without thought. Unnecessary, probably, because no one here would recognize him. And surely nobody would remember what happened over five years ago in Dalton, a town two hours to the south.

Even if someone did remember the old newspaper headlines, he was using a different last name—Coughlin. A name spelled differently enough that no record search would associate him with his past. Yet, on the slim chance that he might encounter someone he'd once known in these parts, it sounded close enough to his real surname that they wouldn't notice the difference—and a sloppy signature would cover, as well.

And instead of T.J., he'd be using his middle name, Joe. A simple, unassuming name. To that old man and everyone else here, he would be just another drifter passing through. Unless, perhaps, they noted the painfully new clothes he wore or the prison-pallor of his skin.

Prison. Only his burning need for justice and his little girl's letters had kept him going during his sentence to hell. He'd served time he didn't deserve, and lost his career, his honor, his daughter. If she ever found out where he'd been, he wanted her to know her daddy was innocent.

Satisfaction slid through him as he stopped in front of a big brick home, double-checked the number, then dredged up a smile and hoped it looked real.

He needed to find the Ricardo Torres gang and finally take them down. But first, he needed to figure out who'd set him up so he could clear his name.

And whether she knew it or not, Abby Hilliard held the key.

"I *REALLY* DON'T WANT purple eye shadow, honey. How about something…" Abby tapped a forefinger against her lips. "Pink? Or green?"

Cocking her head to the side, five-year-old Lindsey Kennedy squinted one eye and surveyed Abby's face with the concentration of a young Michelangelo.

"How 'bout one of each?"

Abby stifled a groan. "At least let me match.

What will your mom think when she gets home?
Or Fred?''

"Please? You'd look real pretty,'' the child
wheedled. "'Specially with your red hair.''

With her straight blond hair and big green eyes,
she could have been a child model if she'd lived
in an urban community instead of such an isolated
town. But her disabled mother struggled to stay
afloat from one week to the next, and modeling
lessons would be an impossible extravagance. Until they'd moved in here, Lindsey and her mom had
been living in a homeless shelter in Winthrop.
Those facts alone made it difficult for Abby to say
no to something so inconsequential.

"All right…but not too dark, okay?''

"'Kay.'' Her forehead furrowed, Lindsey liber-
ally dabbed at the eye-shadow compact and swept
the applicator across Abby's lids. "There,'' she
said with satisfaction. "Just like on TV.''

Like a cartoon, no doubt. Lindsey was entranced
with dressing up and playing with cosmetics, and
today Abby had made a game of putting away toys
with the promise of a makeup session if everything
was done in ten minutes. She'd expected a little
blush, maybe. Perhaps some lip gloss. But Lindsey
had been having so much fun that they'd both gotten a little silly.

From the backyard came the sound of Hamlet's

deep baying. At the first resonant note, Abby jumped to her feet and hurried across the kitchen to the back door. "Excuse me, honey—I've got to get him, or Mrs. Foley will be over here."

Lindsey tagged along. "How come she doesn't like us?"

It was true. The woman hadn't shared a kind word since Abby had moved into this drafty old mausoleum a year ago. And when Abby had started taking in boarders, the woman had become downright hostile. "I think most people would be disturbed by such a loud dog, don't you?" Abby held the back screen door wide and let Hamlet amble in.

No matter how vocal he might be over some exciting event outside, the basset hound's fastest gait was a rolling, bowlegged walk, with his ears dragging on the floor and an ever-sorrowful expression in his droopy eyes, and he'd never summoned the energy to escape the broken-down fence around the backyard.

Now, at Abby's feet, he lifted his large head and bayed once more at full volume. The glassware in the cupboard rattled.

"Hamlet!"

He gave her a reproachful look on his way to his water dish in the corner.

"Maybe he was scared outside," Lindsey observed. "You know, like maybe there were big dogs or something." The makeup session forgotten, she started to scramble down from her chair. "Or maybe there—"

On the way down, her elbow connected with her half-eaten bowl of cereal. The bowl teetered wildly and tipped toward the edge of the counter.

Abby caught it in midair, milk and soggy flakes sloshing against her burgundy fleece pullover and splattering across her newly waxed kitchen floor.

Hamlet did a quick about-face—he always moved a little faster when food was involved—and began licking the floor.

Lindsey stared, her eyes widened with horror. "I'm sorry!"

"It's nothing I can't clean up, honey. You just stay on your chair for a minute, okay?" She retrieved a mop and bucket from the utility closet next to the back door. "I'll take care of this and then we—" From the front hallway came the sound of someone knocking.

Abby blew the bangs out of her eyes as she strode through the formal dining room and into the wide entryway. Beyond the double doors fitted with leaded glass, she could see the silhouette of a tall, broad-shouldered man. *Damn. Not again.*

Setting her jaw, she flung open the door and jammed one hand on her hip.

"Look, I really don't think—" A sense of disorientation gripped her. *"Oh."*

The man outside was definitely not Mrs. Foley's obnoxious son, and he seemed to be more than a little surprised, as well.

He took a step back to look at the brass numerals above the door. "I'm sorry," he said, giving her a wry smile. "I must be at the wrong house."

Realization dawned. "Are you the guy who called about the room yesterday? I'm Abby. It's still available, if you'd like to see it."

He stared back at her. "You're Abby *Hilliard?*"

"Yes, and you are…?"

"Coughlin. Joe Coughlin."

Glancing ruefully at her cereal-spattered pullover, she remembered the mismatched eye shadow. The copious amounts of blush. The eyebrow pencil. The mop in her hand.

With his dark, wavy hair and chiseled features, the man standing on her front step looked as if he'd just stepped out of some soap opera, and she had to look like someone straight out of Comedy Central.

Small footsteps came up behind her, followed by the clicking of Hamlet's toenails across the hardwood floor. She looked down to see Hamlet, with cereal flakes stuck to the top of his nose, and

Lindsey, with bright circles of red on her cheeks and bold, clown-style eyebrows.

No surprise, then, that she caught a flash of confusion in the man's silvery blue eyes. "We've... been playing," she explained. "Would you like to come in?"

"Uh...sure. Why not." He stepped inside and glanced around the ornate moldings rimming the ceilings. The elaborate chandelier sparkling overhead. His gaze stalled on the tent made of blankets over the dining-room chairs, and the walker parked by the coat closet. His expression was that of a man who'd inadvertently stepped into some sort of time warp. "Quite a place you have here," he said faintly. "You...have *boarders?*"

"Well, yes. Isn't that why you came?" Caution flashed through her when she took a closer look at the man she'd just ushered into her home.

His pristine T-shirt was molded tightly over his broad, sculpted chest and upper arms. His jeans were dark indigo and clearly new, as well, hugging narrow hips and heavily muscled thighs.

If he wasn't a bodybuilder, he had to be an outdoor laborer—except he was winter pale instead of tanned by the bright April sunshine. The guys she'd seen yesterday on the road-construction crews outside of town had been working shirtless and were already bronze.

"Some of my other boarders will be here any minute," she added pointedly, resting a protective hand on Lindsey's shoulder and pushing the child behind her. "In fact, *all* of them will."

His eyes were gentle as he held his hands out, palms up. "I've been working my way west, ma'am. I could use a room for a few months. If I find a decent job, I might stay a little longer...then I'll be moving on."

He was a drifter, then. A modern-day hobo without a future. And maybe one with a dark and dangerous past. The lifestyle sent up red flags, even as she thought wistfully of a life so carefree that he could go anywhere, anytime, with nothing holding him back. "I don't allow drugs here. No alcohol, no smoking, no guests of the opposite sex. No loud radios or TV."

"Not a problem."

"Do you have references?"

He hesitated for just a split second. "I've got an 800 number for Williams Concrete. I was there for four years until my back gave out." Reaching into his back pocket, he pulled out a thin wallet and extracted a faded business card worn soft at the edges. "Call him."

"And if my buddy at the sheriff's office checks you out, your record will be clean?"

"Oh, yes, ma'am. Absolutely."

Something about this guy made her feel wary. Still, that last room had been vacant for three months now, and she needed the money. Her heart had gone out to each of her other boarders' plights, and she'd ended up giving every one of them significant discounts. Her brother-in-law, Gene, persistently called them her "charity cases." With this room rented at a full rate, perhaps she could finally make ends meet.

"Okay," she said finally. "Come in and have a cup of coffee while I check your references."

In the kitchen she waved him over to the clawfoot table in the corner, grateful that Hamlet had licked up the cereal disaster on the floor, and poured him a cup of coffee. At the undisguised longing in the man's eyes for the chocolate-chip cookies cooling on the counter, she scooped a half-dozen onto a plate and set it in front of him.

They were gone before she finished her call to the cement contractor. He and Lindsey polished off the next half-dozen while she talked to the sheriff's office.

"Well," she said, cradling the phone, "I guess you check out okay. I'm sorry to seem so suspicious, but I'm responsible for everyone who lives here."

He took a last swallow of coffee and set the cup aside. "Then that makes me feel safer, too."

"Right." Somehow, she couldn't imagine anyone challenging this guy and getting away with
it—he looked as if he could take on any of the
rowdies who hung around the taverns downtown.
Maybe all of them, at one time. Mrs. Foley's son
would be a piece of cake, and that thought made
her smile. "Want to see the room?"

With Lindsey leading the way, she walked ahead
of him up the curved oak staircase to the open
balcony, where she gestured down the hall to the
right. "The first room is the bathroom. The next
room down belongs to Fred, and the one after that
is Catherine's."

"That wouldn't be Fred of Fred's taxi service,
would it?"

She laughed. "One and the same. Though there
isn't much use for taxis in a town of eight thousand."

"My mom and me are at the end," Lindsey
piped up, skipping to the end of the hall. "We've
two rooms with a door between."

"You'll be over here to the left, past the bathroom," Abby continued. She ushered him into the
room and flipped on the light, thankful that she'd
been here earlier today to dust with lemon oil and
open the windows to the fresh breeze. "This one
was once the master bedroom, so there's a nice
sitting room with a desk and daybed, plus a private

half bath. That's why this one is a little more expensive.''

He nodded in approval at the antique brass four-poster and bright quilt.

''Very nice. You and your daughter have a lovely home.''

''*She's* not my mom,'' Lindsey piped up, coming back to stand by Abby. ''Sue is.''

Joe glanced between them. ''I thought…''

''Nope, I was never that blessed,'' Abby said lightly. She ruffled Lindsey's hair. ''I just help Sue with this one whenever I can. Oh—and my rooms are upstairs.''

Lindsey darted to the door next to the bathroom and opened it wide. ''She's up in the treetops. It's *really* cool up there.''

''In the attic?''

Abby gave a dry laugh. ''I prefer to think of it as the penthouse. Really, I believe those rooms were servants' quarters at one time, but they serve my purpose very well. So, what do you think? Do you want the room?'' She quoted him a price, with breakfast and dinner, or without, and held her breath.

''The room is great,'' he said slowly. ''I'd like it. But until I get a job around these parts, maybe I could work off half of my room and board?''

Abby's heart fell as her vision of financial security faded. "Work it off?"

He gave an uncomfortable lift of his shoulder. "For a while. I noticed your bushes need pruning, and that fence around the place needs repair. I can do a little carpentry and painting..."

Earlier, he'd mentioned his injured back, and now she realized that he probably didn't have much money at all, if he was homeless and unable to do manual labor. His wallet had looked awfully thin.

So here was another lost soul, just like the rest of her boarders.

But Sue's MS was in remission now. She'd been feeling stronger lately, able to work more hours at the library. Fred was doing better with his little business, and Catherine hadn't taken a bus trip to the racetracks or casinos in Colorado for almost two months. Given the chance and a little support, people could often find their feet and make a good life for themselves.

"I wouldn't want you doing anything that would hurt your back again," she said firmly. "You'd have to promise to be careful."

"No problem. Maintenance jobs are nothing like concrete work, believe me. I've also had a few years to recover."

She offered her hand. ''We'll give this a month and see how it works out. Deal?''

He smiled and accepted her hand. ''Deal.''

The strong, warm fingers curling around her own were capable, confident—not those of someone who was down on his luck and hoping for reprieve. But more than that, his touch sent a shiver of awareness through her that had no place in a situation like this.

What had she gotten herself into?

CHAPTER TWO

HE'D INTENDED to check out the glamorous Mrs. Hilliard and carefully begin investigating her past. He'd never expected to end up living in her house. He'd also never expected to find her so... interesting. Even with all the garish makeup, he could see she was pretty, with expressive hazel eyes and delicately arched eyebrows.

The photograph clipped from a society page of the newspaper bore little resemblance to the woman herself.

Where were the diamonds, the cold elegance? And she wasn't as tall as he'd guessed, though high heels and a low camera angle could account for that. There'd even been a merry twinkle in her eyes when she'd bantered with the little girl.

If she'd been involved in her late husband's activities, that twinkle would disappear fast enough when she found herself staring at prison walls during a fifteen-to-twenty-year sentence. Though now, after meeting her, the thought didn't fill him with the same sense of satisfaction that it had before.

Almost dizzy with exhaustion after the anxiety and anticipation of being released from Coldwater Penitentiary yesterday, followed by that twelve-hour bus trip, he kicked off his shoes and stretched out on the incredibly soft, comfortable bed in his room and stared at the ceiling.

Instead of a bare bulb in a stark, wire cage, the light fixture was composed of multiple bulbs set into a small version of the chandelier downstairs. There were sparkles in the textured ceiling, as well.

It was so beautiful, such a jarring change from all he'd seen and done and suffered, that his heart swelled until it was almost hard to breathe. He'd lost so much…his sense of reality. His friends. His reputation.

And worst of all, years of his daughter's child-hood…

When he awoke hours later, disoriented and drowsy, late-afternoon shadows were lengthening across the burnished oak floor.

He rose and snagged his duffel, then dumped his sparse wardrobe onto the bed—a few pairs of jeans, some shirts, a single pair of khakis, and a worn LL Bean sweater he'd found at a thrift store while waiting for the Greyhound—and put them in the oak dresser. Not a bad cover, he thought wryly—secondhand clothes and arrival by bus.

In another pocket of the duffel bag were the

items he wouldn't have wanted anyone to see—his small laptop, a palm-size digital camera, a tiny tape recorder and a set of manila files. He stowed the bag on the highest shelf in the dark, cramped closet.

The equipment had been waiting at a post office not far from the state penitentiary, sent by over-night mail courtesy of his older brother, Carl, in California. The cement company employment reference for Joe Coughlin was courtesy of Carl, as well. Unless someone delved into Joe's income tax records, that cover would hold, as would the false identity he'd set up before coming here.

Once he cleared his name, he'd go to Carl's to retrieve his daughter and his possessions, access his savings accounts and start his life over. Not with the DEA, certainly…not after the way his for-mer buddies had stabbed him in the back. But he'd be able to make a clean start in something simi-lar…like opening a security firm, maybe.

Heaven knew, he'd learned enough in prison to thwart ninety percent of the bastards out on the streets.

At a soft rap on his door, he spun around and crouched, every sense tuned to self-protection. Catching himself quickly, he straightened and took a steadying breath. *Thank God the door is shut.*

He'd already seen the suspicion in Abby Hilliard's eyes when he'd first arrived. If she and her friend at the sheriff's office dug a little deeper...

He opened the door a few inches, blocking it from opening farther with one foot, only to find Lindsey peering up at him with solemn eyes. "Abby says it's time to eat. And you're late."

"I'll be down in a minute." He glanced at his wristwatch. "I thought dinner was at six o'clock."

"Nope, 'cause this is her school night."

"School? She teaches *school?*"

"Nope. She goes, like me." The child gave him a big smile. "And she's even *old.*"

Not old at all, from what he'd learned during his Internet search. Just thirty. But with the significant amount of money she must have inherited from her late husband, why was she going to school?

Given this grand old house and the kind of cash her husband must have had lying around, she could be sunning herself in Cancún right now or seeing the sights in Europe. Yet here she was, in Podunk, U.S.A. And with *boarders?*

Locking his door behind him, he followed the little girl down the wide staircase and into the dining room. He faltered at the doorway as a sense of unreality slid through him.

He'd had his last meal twenty-four hours ago, seated at a hundred-foot steel table, shoulder to shoulder with fellow inmates wearing identical grays. To inadvertently disrespect someone—to even brush another guy's arm while reaching for the pepper—meant trouble. Speaking to the wrong guy guaranteed it. And the food...his stomach pitched at the memory.

Here, four faces turned toward him with expressions of acceptance and welcome. A linen tablecloth covered the table, for God's sake. A *tablecloth.* There was a platter of fried chicken with curls of steam rising above it, surrounded by bowls of parsley-buttered potatoes and carrots. An incredible yeasty aroma of freshly baked dinner rolls filled the air.

He hadn't had a hot meal in five years. No matter what the menu, his food had inevitably been cold. There'd never been enough. And none of it had ever, ever smelled this good.

But just looking at these people—these normal, everyday people—made him uneasy as he struggled to remember the kind of small talk they would expect. If he'd just arrived from Mars, he couldn't have felt more inept.

"You look like you haven't eaten in a week," Abby said dryly as she lit a candle in the center of the table. She nodded toward an empty chair. "Come on in and let me introduce you."

Giving himself a mental shake, Joe shuffled into the room. "Fred and I have met."

The old man's eyes narrowed. "Guess we did. Maybe you and I'll need to have a good long talk one of these days, eh?"

"Fred!" At the far end of the table, an elderly woman sniffed and stiffened her spine. "At least try to be polite to the poor man." She directed a prim smile in Joe's direction. "Fred's always suspicious of newcomers, especially those who move in here, I'm Catherine Martin. We certainly do hope you enjoy your stay."

Fred muttered something unintelligible, and the look he darted toward Catherine could have halted a locomotive in its tracks.

From her chair next to Joe, a pale woman with thick glasses and dark hair pulled back into a ponytail gave him a faint smile. "I'm Sue," she said, her voice barely audible. "I guess you've met my daughter already."

There were lines of tension around her eyes and she held herself awkwardly, as if she might be in pain. Lindsey slid into the chair next to her, and gave her mother's arm a gentle pat. "She's got headaches," the child explained in a stage whisper. "So we have to be real quiet."

"I'm fine, honey," her mother murmured. "Really."

Joe nodded a greeting to them all as he took his place. He'd just reached for his fork when he realized that they'd all bowed their heads and were reciting a table prayer.

He hadn't heard one in years.

"So," Catherine said after the food had been passed and everyone was eating, "where are you from?"

He wondered what they would say if they knew. "Colorado." He'd once lived there for a while. Every place since then was better left unsaid.

"I have a sister who's lived in Colorado for thirty years. I go see her quite a bit." Fred squinted at him from across the table. "What town are you from?"

"Colorado Springs." When the old man's eyes lit up, Joe knew the guy was planning to quiz him on it, so he added smoothly, "Where does your sister live?"

"Rural, to the east. Ranch country. Prettiest land you'll ever see. Why, I remember—"

"And what do you do, Mr. Coughlin?" Catherine interrupted, arching an eyebrow at the old man. "We'd love to hear about it."

"Some ranch work…construction…but after my divorce, nothing seemed to matter anymore. I just started drifting."

"It must have been so hard for you," Sue murmured.

All eyes were on him, filled with such sympathy

that his fabrication settled uneasily in his stomach. There'd be less sympathy if they knew the truth—that he'd given the long hours and dangers of his DEA career a far higher priority than his family. He'd been a selfish bastard.

"I'm okay now. Really. I'm heading toward my brother's place in California."

Fred studied him. "So how long will you be here?"

"A few months, maybe longer." He gestured toward the windows, where the distant Rockies rose like a pale blue sawtooth edge along the horizon.

"Beautiful area you've got here."

"We all love it." Abby ate a few bites and then picked up her plate. "I'd better get moving. Is your room all right?"

The wild makeup was gone now, replaced with just mascara and a light touch of blush. He'd been right—she was one very pretty woman. Not that looks couldn't deceive.

He'd arrested a guy in Cheyenne who'd had long white hair and the merriest smile he'd ever seen—a Santa clone if there ever was one—and there'd been a twenty-pound stash of meth in the guy's car.

"The room is fine. I hope you're coming up with a list of things for me to do here."

"The problem," she retorted, "will be deciding which you'll have time for. I could keep you busy for the next year."

LONG AFTER POSSIBLY the best meal in his entire life, after Abby had taken off for Winthrop with a backpack of textbooks and the others had disappeared into their rooms or gathered around the television in the living room, Joe stood out on the porch and stared out into the night.

Though it clearly needed significant maintenance, this house was one of the biggest of the grand dames of the avenue—with the red brick, leaded glass and interior woodwork of a home that would have belonged to the wealthy. So where had Oren Hilliard's money gone?

Even more interesting, one of the Sheltering Pines funeral homes stood right next door. There were four of them scattered through this part of the state, and the ones he'd seen boasted the same level of architectural grandeur, with towering white pillars in front and lacy gingerbread at the eaves and cornices. Like Abby's house, they were all constructed of dark red brick.

His search into suspicious financial matters at the funeral home down in Dalton years ago had turned up a hell of a lot more than he'd expected, leading him straight to the Torres gang. He'd been after them for a long, long time and had gotten so close…then within days, five kilos of meth appeared in his car and a squadron of armed police officers appeared at his door.

Perhaps there were documents in this house…or in the funeral home next door. Names. Phone numbers. Records of some sort. If there were, he would find them, and nail the guys who'd set him up. Then he would bring down the money-laundering operation that had set this all in motion.

And if Abby and her brother-in-law, Gene, were still carrying on the proud family tradition of crime, he would send them to prison, too.

GENE HILLIARD BOWED his head respectfully as Mrs. Langley dabbed the tears from her eyes. "You can take comfort from knowing that Edgar planned his funeral," he murmured. "He made the final payment several months ago."

She sniffled into a tissue. "We b-both made our funeral plans here, but it's been such a long time. C-can I go take a look at the caskets again?"

"Of course, of course." He shot a quick glance at the clock as he reached over to rest a solicitous hand on hers. "Or would you rather wait until tomorrow? Maybe your daughter will be in town by then. I'd guess that she'd like to be here with you during this most difficult time."

"Oh…well, maybe so…" She raised her troubled, watery gaze to his.

"You're open on Sundays?"

"When there's a need, of course. We want to do anything we can to help you."

She cast a doubtful look toward the door leading into the casket display room. "Well…I suppose I'd better wait, then. You've been wonderful through all of this, Gene."

He gave her a small, caring smile. "It's our job here at Sheltering Pines."

When she finally rose to her feet, he gently took her arm and guided her to the front door, noting with satisfaction that she still drove a late-model Lincoln. She and her husband had done well over the years. They'd always preferred the best, and fortunately, they'd paid for it right to the last.

They'd both opted for the solid mahogany Model 2349, plus a triple-reinforced bronze vault, and he'd barely had to start his usual pitch.

He locked the door and strolled back into the building, turning off the lights as he went. Back in the display room, he turned on the lights and felt a familiar wave of satisfaction slide through him.

In the woods section, mahogany and oak and cherry high-gloss finishes gleamed, while over in the metals, his favorite casket of all—a solid bronze—glowed under strategically placed spot-lights.

The cheaper ones were farther in back under stark fluorescent lights, but these... He breathed a sigh of contentment as he wound his way through the display. These were so beautiful that some-times he came in just to glide his hand along the mirrorlike top-coating of the higher-priced models, or to brush his fingers across the soft velvet and satin linings.

Of course, with his 800 percent markup on the more luxurious models, that beauty was infinitely enhanced.

A tasteful vellum card rested against the white velvet or taffeta interior of each style, indicating the price and model number. He reached the casket model the Langleys had chosen, lifted out the card and switched it with a card from a less expensive model farther down the line.

It had been a number of years, after all. Mrs. Langley would hardly remember the details when she came in tomorrow, and old Edgar sure couldn't come back to complain about being laid to rest in a cheaper casket. As long as the model numbers on the card matched the contract, the grieving widow would be satisfied.

With a last, contented glance around the room,

Gene flicked off the lights and headed upstairs to the small night duty apartment he occasionally used.

Godiva met him at his door, her fluffy white tail twitching and her emerald-green eyes slitted with annoyance. "Here, sweetheart," he cooed, leaning over with outstretched hands.

The cat's tail raised in a shepherd's crook, she marched haughtily into the small efficiency kitchen, clearly miffed over her late dinner and the cramped surroundings.

He chuckled fondly as he followed her to the refrigerator. She favored the lovely bay window of his house at the east end of town on Boulder Street, where she could sit like the princess she was and observe any passersby.

"You'll be back home tomorrow, darling," he murmured.

His amusement faded when he noticed the light blinking on his answering machine. His heart sank when he saw the number on the caller ID.

With trembling fingers he pushed the Listen button.

"You know who this is, Gene. And you know why we're calling. Tomorrow, man. And remember—don't be late."

The cat forgotten, he sank into the closest chair, tipped his head back and closed his eyes.

And tried not to think about what would happen to him if he failed to follow through.

"I JUST NEVER DREAMED this would ever to happen to Bonnie." Carl's voice broke. "But at least you're out, now. You can take Megan this week?"

"Of course." Bringing his daughter back into his life right now wasn't ideal. Just one more month would have helped. But there were no other relatives who could take her, and during Joe's years in hell, Carl had done more than anyone had a right to ask. "You've got enough to worry about."

"I'm sorry, buddy. We wanted to let her stay here so she could get to know you again gradually. It would have been better that way."

"Did you ever tell her the truth about me?"

Carl sighed heavily. "No, I did just what you wanted me to. But maybe that was worse. We told her you were on business far away and couldn't come back—we even addressed her letters. That's probably why she's so angry—she thinks you could have come for her after Sheri and her husband died, and figures you just didn't care. If we only had more time…"

Memories flashed through Joe's mind. The fights with Sheri over his erratic DEA hours. The weeks of bitter silence. The divorce—and her almost immediate remarriage to someone who'd apparently been waiting in the wings. Since then he'd second-guessed his decisions too many times to count, wondering if his marriage might have survived if he'd given up his career.

If Sheri would still be alive.

Joe leaned his head against the wall of the convenience store as a familiar wave of guilt and pain washed through him. "I just don't know what to say. It's all beyond fixing—and it's all my fault."

"No," Carl said firmly. "That's not true at all."

Joe glanced around, suddenly uncomfortable. He'd walked to a pay phone by a convenience store to call Carl, away from any eavesdroppers at the boardinghouse, but now he felt hesitant to say much in such a public place. Ten feet away, customers were strolling in and out of the store.

Some of them eyed him with the blatant curiosity of small-town residents who rarely see a stranger in their midst. Others glanced at his ragged denim jacket and battered Nikes—two new acquisitions from the thrift store down the street—and gave a little shudder.

He didn't blame them, though the other jacket options had been well worn and emblazoned with logos like Erwin's Hog Farm and Mighty Grow Seed Corn, and those jackets had made *him* shudder. The shoes had been the only ones that fit, looked fairly new and were—hopefully—clean.

"I'm really sorry about Bonnie," he murmured, keeping his voice low. "Is she going to pull through this?"

"We're praying. She's got several more rounds of chemo to go, and then radiation after that. Her surgery went well, but the first round of chemo really knocked her for a loop."

"She's a wonderful woman, Carl. I owe you both more than I can ever repay."

"It's breaking her heart, thinking about sending Megan away. Your girl has been like another daughter. But our four are going to stay with Bonnie's mother for a month. She's eighty and she's worried she can't even handle that many children. And with what Bonnie's been going through…"

The pain in his brother's voice was palpable. Joe cut in. "Look, I've been planning to buy some old junker for a few hundred bucks, to hold me over until I can pick up my Blazer at your place. I'll find a set of wheels as soon as I can and be on my way."

"I've got a week of vacation coming. You said you're still in Wyoming—I can bring your SUV and Megan to you and then fly home."

"No—I'll just come to your house and pick them both up, and save you the trouble."

"Then let's meet partway. I'll enjoy the drive and having a few hours alone with Megan. Our place is always so crazy, it's hard to have a quiet conversation. Maybe I can help make her transition easier."

"But Bonnie—"

"Her friend Judy can stay with her for the day." Carl gave an uncomfortable chuckle. "I should have been there waiting for you when you got out. If you would have just told me sooner, I could have gotten your things out of storage and asked for the time off."

"I didn't know myself until the day before my release. My new lawyer had been working on this for a long time, but after the judge threw out my conviction on a technicality, everything happened fast."

"About time." Carl's voice filled with righteous indignation. "They finally found you innocent after all?"

"Not exactly. My attorney discovered there'd been illegal search and seizure of evidence—and a falsified signature on the warrant."

"Can they retry your case?"

"One of the witnesses has died, and the other one recanted. A new forensics expert says the fingerprint match is inconclusive. The district attorney has announced that there won't be a new trial.''

"But they didn't really clear your name, then." Carl gave a disgusted snort. "What's wrong with those fools?"

"At least this got me back out on the street. Now I can finally take care of this myself."

Carl sucked in a breath. "Leave it alone. Move out here. I'll find you a good job, and you can just leave all that behind."

"I can't."

"What about Megan? What's fair to her now that her mother's dead?" Carl's voice rose on a pleading note. "You're dealing with dangerous people, here. What if you get killed?"

Anger, frustration and a growing sense of hopelessness had gnawed at him as Joe's years of incarceration passed, threatening to consume him. What he'd had to do to survive had gone against almost every principle he'd lived by before the day the gates locked behind him. And now he wouldn't be able to take a true breath of freedom until he took down those responsible for putting him there.

"I can find out who did it, Carl. I was getting too close to something big."

After a heavy silence, Carl sighed. "We'd better keep Megan here, then."

Longing, so pure and sharp that it made his eyes

burn, filled Joe's chest. He'd wanted her to believe that her father was just…away…so he'd refused to let Carl bring her to Wyoming for visitations at the pen. He'd hoped Megan's little friends would never hear the truth and be cruel to her.

But Carl had forwarded mail from her, and Joe knew how much his absence had hurt her. He'd read her misspelled notes from first grade, when she'd awkwardly printed, *DONT YOU LOVE ME? PLESE COM HOME.*

In second grade, she'd written, *I miss my mommy. She's in heaven, and I need you. Why won't you come back?*

By third grade she'd been more eloquent, but the message hadn't changed.

Last summer, she'd stopped writing. Maybe she'd forgotten him…or simply didn't care. The adjustment was going to be hard on her when he reappeared in her life.

"Look—I've been here almost a week. Megan will be safe. These people don't know who I am, and a woman here might know something I can use. It won't take me long—a month, maybe—and then Megan and I will move to Sacramento."

"I don't know…"

"There's still some money in that money-market account I set up for her, right? Take out enough for your expenses—your flight back, motels, anything. There aren't any rental places here, but I could take a bus to Reno. That wouldn't be more than what—a couple of hours from your place? You could leave early in the morning and be home the same day, so you wouldn't need to be away from Bonnie as long. Just spend a few hours with me so Megan can adjust a little.''

''I just wish…''

''We'll manage.'' Joe looked down at the calendar on his watch. ''How about Sunday the twentieth? Can you get ready to go in a few days?''

It took another five minutes to arrange the meeting place—the parking lot of a motel on the edge of Reno—and to discuss the other necessary details. Afterward, Joe leaned against the bricks and closed his eyes briefly.

During his years in prison, he'd had a lot of time to plan his investigation. He'd known it would be difficult, but now he needed to take his daughter away from the only home she'd known for years. A daughter who would despise him even more when she found out why he hadn't been able to be a part of her life.

Between the Torres gang and his ten-year-old girl, he knew the gang was going to be far easier to face.

CHAPTER THREE

"YOU LOOK LOVELY tonight, my dear." Gene rested a proprietary hand at the small of Abby's back as they made their way through the crowd at the Twelfth Annual Silver Springs Rescue Society Fund-raiser.

The feel of his fleshy hand at her waist, even through the layers of her velvet shawl and black silk cocktail dress, made her skin crawl. His casual endearment made her cringe. "I should be home studying," she whispered. "One hour, and I'm out of here."

His hand tightened on her shawl and dress, pulling her to a halt, as he reached in front of her face to shake hands with the mayor. "Great turnout, don't you think, sir? We ought to easily top last year's achievement. You've done a fabulous job."

The mayor turned to give Gene a satisfied nod, then his gaze slid down to meet Abby's. His smile turned genuine. "We do appreciate the support. Seeing everyone at this event each year does my heart good. Last year, Sheltering Pines's donation made it possible to add six new dog runs for strays.'' He winked at her. ''And it seems to me that you went home with a new friend, as well.''

''That would be Hamlet,'' she agreed. ''But this year I'm not—''

A woman on the other side of the room waved at him. ''Mayor!''

He started back through the crowd. ''Best of luck on the bidding!'' he called over his shoulder. ''We have some wonderful offerings this year.''

''That's what I'm afraid of,'' she muttered. ''As long as they don't have fur, fins or feathers, I'll consider it. Otherwise, I'm out of here.''

''Smile, dammit. I ask very little of you,'' Gene retorted, his voice low. ''These events are *important*.''

She remembered well, because her late husband, Oren, had felt the same way. He'd belonged to every civic organization in town, sang in the church choir, stayed on the City Planning Commission for three terms. Anything and everything he could do to be a visible presence in community affairs. He'd always said it was his duty.

She'd always suspected it was more self-serving than that—a business tool he used to inspire confidence and drum up business in one fell swoop.

Louise Shaeffer, the floral designer who worked part-time at the funeral home and lived just across the street, drifted up in a diaphanous pink gown. In her midfifties, but already a little hard-of-hearing, she still dyed her hair platinum blond and loved to dress up as if for prom night at every opportunity.

She gripped Abby's hands with both of her own. "I saw the most *interesting* man leaving your house this morning. Couldn't have been much past six o'clock." Her mouth lifted into a secretive grin. "A friend of yours? He was positively *gorgeous.*"

"Now, what were you doing outside at six?" Abby fought the urge to roll her eyes. If she ever did have an affair, she certainly wouldn't have the guy leave by the front door, because the rest of the town would hear the news in minutes.

Louise laughed. "Well, I was getting my paper out on the porch, and there he was. Black leather… big shoulders…strolling down the street like he owned the world. I just love that kind of confidence in a man, don't you?"

"He's not my 'friend.' He's a temporary boarder," Abby explained patiently, hoping Louise was listening. "Just that. Nothing more." She met the older woman's eyes dead-on. "*Nothing.*"

"But he had some sort of carry-on bag. I thought—"

Abby sighed. "His *duffel* bag. He told me he's

going to be gone overnight, to pick up his car and his young daughter.''

Surprising news, really—he'd essentially said he was a drifter, just a guy casually working his way back west. He hadn't said anything about having a child. What kind of man would disappear from his child's life like that?

Not an honorable one. Not a man who had character. Abby suppressed a shudder.

Louise, however, pursed her lips and nodded as if satisfied. ''He's probably been in the service. Or maybe he's one of those guys who does construction down south during the winter and then heads back north come spring?'' She gazed expectantly at Abby.

''I...well...''

''Excuse us, Louise,'' Gene said, once again placing his hand at Abby's waist. ''There's someone over by the punch bowl we need to see.''

Instead of heading for the table laden with appetizers and beverages, he steered Abby to one side. ''Do you see what happens, with you taking in all of those people?'' he hissed. ''The community talks. It appears that Sheltering Pines isn't doing well if you keep taking in lodgers. It also compromises your reputation.''

She stepped away from his hand and glared at

him. "I wouldn't need to if Oren's estate hadn't been so tangled."

"You received your proper share of the business," he said coldly. "And now, though you take no responsibility for running it, you receive what you are owed each month."

Knowing it wouldn't make a difference, she refrained from pointing out that he had refused her offer to help with the books. "Which just about covers keeping up that relic of a house I received, heating it and paying my tuition."

"The tuition is a ridiculous waste. You could come into the business. Answer the phone. Deal with mourners. You could even do the florals, and save me from paying Louise."

"We've had this discussion before. I do appreciate the offer, but I'm not interested. Finishing my degree is important to me." *And so is a career far away from here.*

From the other side of the room came the cheery voice of the administrator of the local nursing home, announcing the start of the auction. The mayor stepped up onto the platform and stood next to her with an antique velvet quilt draped over his arms.

The raucous, rapid-fire voice of the auctioneer filled the air.

Giving Gene a curt nod, Abby stepped around

him and joined the gathering crowd, slipping between several couples and moving ahead so Gene couldn't follow.

Though he'd never said anything suggestive to her, she'd avoided him for years because he irritated her to no end. Worse, he'd deemed himself her guardian after Oren's death, never hesitating to criticize or provide unwanted advice. Just the sight of Gene's car made her head turn in the opposite direction.

And now, thanks to a complex estate involving the four Sheltering Pines funeral homes and various other investments, she was also financially tied to him.

Even the house she lived in, though it was specifically willed for her use, could not be sold without Gene's consent. It was part of the business, and he owned the controlling shares.

The neighboring town had a good college, though, so the house was useful now. Once she finished school, she'd finally have a good career. She'd find a good lawyer to deal with Gene, and she would be on her way.

Graduation could not come soon enough.

EARLY SATURDAY, Joe boarded the bus to Reno. Tired and cramped when he arrived, he shouldered his duffel bag and considered a taxi, then decided to walk. What was the point of racing to that parking lot and then waiting for hours? And walking gave him time to think.

He hadn't seen his daughter for over five years—not since the last time he'd visited her just before being arrested. What would she be like now? Carl had sent photographs every few months, but at ten years of age she'd look different, act different than the beautiful little preschooler he'd last seen. And she probably wouldn't remember a thing about her dad.

Would she be frightened? Would she even be willing to come with him—or would she become hysterical and cling to Carl, begging him to take her back to California? And what could he say to make things easier?

He already knew she was upset over his failure to visit her, but until he finished his business in Silver Springs, he hoped she wouldn't find out where he'd been. If she inadvertently shared that information with the wrong person, it could destroy his chance to track down the guys who'd betrayed him. Worse, it would tip off the drug traffickers he still hoped to find.

Which left Joe with the prospect of lying to his little girl.

After shaving and changing his clothes in a gas station rest room, Joe found the motel and settled down on a bench to wait. Too edgy to eat or to read the book in his duffel bag, he watched the traffic out on the street.

An hour later, Joe's black Blazer pulled into the parking lot with Carl behind the wheel. A stranger—a beautiful young girl—sat beside him, her face a pale, expressionless mask.

Carl flung open the driver's side door, jumped out, and slammed it shut. He rushed forward to envelope Joe in a bear hug, then awkwardly stepped back with the biggest smile Joe had ever seen.

"God, it's so good to see you." Carl's gaze skated briefly to Megan, who sat silently in the car, and his voice lowered. "And finally, without that damn plate glass between us. I've waited and waited for this day!"

"What have you told her?"

Carl chewed on his lower lip. "She knows about the situation at home with Bonnie, and that you are her dad. She was really upset at first, but now she's just sort of...I don't know, stoic." He cleared his throat.

"It's...not the first time she's had to face change. First your divorce...then Sheri's remarriage...then you disappeared...then Sheri and her husband died. She's a pretty tough little thing, after going through all of that. I did promise her that she could come visit us—with you along—real soon.''

''What else?''

Carl grimaced. ''I didn't say anything about where you've been or what you're doing in Silver Springs. She still thinks you've been working out on the East Coast and just couldn't get back. She's old enough to think that's a pretty flimsy excuse, though. Be ready for some tough questions. I also told her that you were going by 'Joe' now, instead of 'T.J.' I said you didn't like your childhood nickname any more now that you're older.'' Carl lowered his voice. ''How are you gonna handle your last name?''

''Cauthen…Coughlin…they sound just about the same, and I sign Coughlin like a doctor would—illegibly. I don't have any bills or magazines coming here, so she'll never see the name on a label. I think I can make it for a couple months.''

Carl nodded, then turned and brace both hands on the open driver's side window of the Blazer. ''Hey, sugar—want some lunch? My plane leaves in three hours. Let's all get to know each other over some pizza, okay?''

This time she barely nodded.

''Come here, Joe, and meet your daughter.'' Beaming like a proud father, Carl rounded the truck and opened her door. "Come on out, honey. Someone really wants to meet you."

She didn't move.

"Come on, Megan. It's time."

She slowly unbuckled her seat belt and climbed out, then stood tightly at Carl's side with her head lowered. It struck Joe that she looked as if she were headed for execution rather than a meeting with her dad, and the immense loss of the years without her weighed like an anvil on his heart. Maybe this wouldn't work—and then what would he do?

"Hi, Megan," he said softly. "I've missed you so much."

She lifted her head, her eyes hot and accusing and scared.

The impact of looking at her—at the dark wavy hair and silvery blue eyes that were exactly like his own—stunned him.

Nearly speechless over the enormity of this moment, he wanted to hug her. Lift her high in the air and twirl her around. Kiss her soft cheek. And she looked as if she wanted him to disappear.

"Well," Carl said with a burst of enthusiasm. "Isn't this great? You two have lots to talk about. But let's do it over a big pizza, okay? I think everyone's tired and hungry here."

MEGAN EYED the stranger—her dad—sitting behind the wheel of the Blazer and scowled, trying to quell the flip-flops that had tied her stomach in knots for the past hour.

Being scared and angry and lonesome all at once had made it impossible to eat at that pizza place. Uncle Carl had been so cheerful, so talkative, that it seemed as if he was *glad* to see her go. And Dad had mostly looked at her with that funny sad expression, as though he felt really bad about taking her away.

Maybe, she thought glumly, he didn't really want her, either.

Now she had to go to the bathroom, and all she could see, for miles around, was *nothing*. Just scrubby-looking plants and sand.

Her stomach growled and she wrapped her arms tighter around her waist, huddling closer to the door.

Uncle Carl would have noticed her, and offered to stop somewhere. He was always ready to pull over for a bathroom break, or ice cream, or a rental movie, or to throw Frisbees in a park. He laughed a lot and liked to tease, and he'd been like a real dad to her.

Feeling a tear slip down her face, she huddled into an even tighter ball, not wanting her dad to see.

"Hey, sugar," he said, sliding a quick glance in

her direction. Above his dark sunglasses she saw his forehead furrow. He bit his lower lip when he turned his eyes back to the empty road ahead. "This isn't easy for you, I know."

She traced the door handle with her forefinger. If she told him how much she hated coming out here, what would he do? Would he yell at her for being a big baby? Drop her off with someone else—or just leave her at the side of the road?

There was nobody else out here. Not a car, not a town, not a single person walking. She'd never be able to find her way back to Uncle Carl and Aunt Bonnie.

"You didn't eat anything back there. I'll bet you're hungry." He reached over behind the seat and lifted up a small cooler, then set it between the two front seats. "I tried to guess what you'd like."

She felt her cheeks heat.

From the corner of her eye, she saw him look at her again. "There's a small town up ahead, probably five or six miles. Do you need to stop?"

She nodded miserably, afraid to speak because her lower lip was already trembling, and if she tried, maybe she'd just start bawling and not be able to quit.

"Do you need to stop sooner?" he asked gently. "We can pull over."

She gave her head a sharp shake.

"You're sure?"

When she managed a quick nod, he reached over and rested his hand on her shoulder for a second before turning his attention back to the road.

"I remember the day you were born," he said. "I couldn't believe it. You were such a beautiful baby, right from the start. The nurses said so, too."

When she didn't answer, he just kept talking in that nice low voice, a voice that sounded as if he could be a radio announcer or someone on TV.

"I was twenty-seven years old then, and I felt like I owned the world, I was so proud. I thought our family was so happy that nothing would ever, ever break us apart. But that's what happened, and then your mom and Leif moved far away—clear to Texas. I didn't get to see you much after that." He gave her a quick glance again and chuckled sadly, as if he couldn't quite believe it. "Do you remember me at all, Megan?"

Did she? Uncertain, she just gave a little shrug. He and Mom had divorced when she was four, and Mom had never talked about him again. He sure hadn't ever bothered to come see her.

Sometimes, though, she had searched out that box in Mom's closet and had hidden herself away so she could look at the pictures inside. There were pictures of herself as a baby, in Mom's arms, with a dark, handsome guy who had to be Dad, though now he looked a lot older. And there were some of her in Dad's arms, too, and he was smiling. Maybe he'd loved her when she was tiny and cute.

"I know things haven't been easy, sugar, losing your mom and stepdad. The accident must have been terrifying for you. And now I'm here, taking you away from your uncle Carl—I just hope I can make it up to you."

What she wanted was to have her old life back, but she knew that was hopeless—and Dad seemed so gentle, so concerned, that she couldn't bring herself to tell him just how bad she felt. Why did everything have to change?

When she looked up and straightened enough to see out the front window, she spotted the outline of some buildings ahead. "Is that the town?"

"It is. We'll stop there, okay? You can run in to use the facilities, and I'll put gas in the car." He drummed his fingers lightly on the steering wheel. "Do you like dogs?"

Surprised, she turned enough to look at him more fully.

"Do you like basset hounds? They're the ones with the big, long floppy ears and the sad eyes."

She nodded.

"Where we're going, they've got a big ole basset hound named Hamlet. And there's a girl there, too. Lindsey's a lot younger than you, but she's a nice little gal.''

''Is she yours?'' Megan asked in a small voice.

''Nope. But she lives there. And there's a funny lady who sometimes gets her makeup put on in *very* unusual ways.'' He smiled, as if he could see her right now. ''The first day I met her, she had green eye shadow on one eye, and pink on the other. *And* she had big red circles on her cheeks—sort of like a clown. And she had cereal all over her shirt.''

Megan tried to imagine Aunt Bonnie doing something like that, and couldn't. She sat up a little straighter. ''Why?''

''I think she was playing a game.''

Some of those nervous knots in her stomach eased a little. ''She sounds kinda nice.'' Ahead, she could see a sign for a gas station. ''We're stopping there?''

''I sure plan to, sugar.''

As soon as he pulled in at a gas pump, he strode into the station and brought out a key, then took her to the right door on the side of the building and waited. When she was finished, she came out and found he was still by the door.

His eyes weren't on her, though. He was watching two creepy guys on a huge silver and black motorcycle who had pulled in on the other side of the pump.

One of them started putting gas in the motorcycle. The one with the scraggly beard pulled a can of beer from a saddlebag, cracked it open and lifted it for a long swallow, then crushed the can in one hand and tossed it on the ground.

He belched and eyed the open windows of Dad's Blazer, then moved a little closer to take a better look.

She stared in growing horror as he reached inside and took something from the glove box.

"Hey, you freakin' loser!" he called out to Dad, his voice harsh. "Whaddaya lookin' at? You got a problem with me?" He glanced at his friend, then swaggered toward the building, a mean look in his eyes. "Pretty little gal you got there. Think she'd like to go for a ride?"

"Hey, man," the other biker called out, his voice impatient. "Don't mess with them. We gotta hit the road."

Ignoring the warning, the guy with the beard kept coming, though now he was staring at the front door of the gas station. "You touch that phone, kid, and you're dead meat. This job of yours ain't worth dyin' over."

"Megan, I want you to go back inside the

ladies' room and lock the door. *Now,*" Dad said in a low voice.

When she just stood rooted to the spot, he put his hands on her shoulders and gently pushed her back into the bathroom. "You stay in there, *no matter what.* You understand? Lock the door. *Promise* me."

He flipped on the light switch and smiled down at her. "Don't worry. I think he just took my wallet, since I was careless enough to leave it in there. I'm going to ask him to give it back. Now *lock the door.*"

He shut the door tight, then she heard him move away. His steps didn't start again until she locked the door with a *snick.*

Fear rushed through her. Those guys with the motorcycle were very, very bad news. What if they hurt Dad or that guy in the station? What if they came after *her?*

She heard Dad's quiet voice, and then one of the other men gave a harsh laugh. Her fear changed to terror when she heard someone swear and the sound of scuffling feet.

Something metal clanged. More shouts came from inside the gas station—though she'd seen the skinny teenager in there, working alone, and knew he wouldn't be any help. What if Dad got shot? Stabbed? What if he was *dying?*

Shivering, she cowered at the back of the filthy room, her heart pounding in her throat and knees turning to rubber.

Something slammed into the ground. Someone moaned. *Dad?*

Sobbing, she rushed to the door and struggled to slide back the lock—afraid to look, afraid not to. Afraid that if she didn't do something—*anything*—he would never stand a chance.

Her entire body shaking, she pried the door open an inch…and then another, trying to see.

She stared in shock.

One biker was doubled up on the ground, his arms wrapped around his stomach. The other was crouched low and moving toward her dad, his arms stretched forward and his teeth bared.

She cried out against her fist as the man rushed forward, his head low and something silver gleaming in his hand.

Her dad, the man who'd so gently asked if she needed the bathroom, who'd talked about the funny lady and the basset hound just minutes earlier, moved so fast that she could barely see what he did.

Now he was somehow behind the biker, with the man's arm wrenched high up behind his back. When the guy dropped to his knees, she saw that Dad had a gun.

It was pressed at the man's throat.

A cold sweat made Megan's shirt stick to her back. All at once she felt dizzy, and faint, and very, very scared.

Sirens wailed up the highway. Closer and closer. Two highway patrol cars pulled to a stop on the gravel, sending clouds of dust and gravel billowing across the parking lot.

When the dust cleared, the bikers were flat on the ground, their hands cuffed behind their backs, and the boy in the gas station was talking to the officers, gesturing wildly with both hands.

Giving up to her fear, she spun around and threw up in the toilet until her heaving stomach couldn't bring up anything else.

There'd been two of those men—big and muscled, and as scary as any bad guys she'd ever seen on TV. Now one of them had blood streaming from his nose, and the other one had a lot of blood on his cheek. And Dad was talking to the two cops as calmly as if he was just talking about the weather.

Uncle Carl had said that it was time for her to go with her dad. He'd said Joe was a good man, and that he loved her, and that he would be a good father.

But what she'd just seen was a man who was nothing like her uncle Carl—he was a fighter, and he was *terrifying,* no matter what anyone said. And all she wanted to do was go back home to her own bedroom right now, where Aunt Bonnie would hug her and Uncle Carl would make her laugh.

Dropping her head to her upraised knees, she began to cry.

THE HOUSE WAS ALWAYS quiet at this time of night. With everyone else asleep, Abby often came downstairs to curl up on the sofa and savor a cup of decaf by the fireplace as she studied for her degree in social work.

At a soft rap on the front door she jerked upright, nearly spilling her coffee, and glanced up at the clock. Who would be knocking at midnight? Uneasy, she moved to the dining-room window where she could stand at just the right angle and see anyone under the front porch light.

A man stood there, with a duffel bag in one hand and a suitcase in the other. She would have recognized Joe's height and broad shoulders anywhere. A child was next to him, her head bowed and shoulders slumped in apparent exhaustion, a cascade of tangled dark curls obscuring her profile.

Ever since Louise's questions at the fund-raiser, Abby's curiosity—and doubts—about Joe had grown, but at the sight of the young girl, her heart melted. Here was a child who needed a warm bed and a good meal.

She hurried to the entryway and opened the locks. "Come in, come in!"

Hamlet brushed against her leg as he came to join her at the door, offering a halfhearted *woof* when she stood aside to usher them in. After a cursory inspection, he lumbered back to his favorite place in the kitchen, where he always kept one eye on the refrigerator.

Joe's daughter just stood there, until he curved a hand behind her shoulders and urged her inside. As soon as she came through the door, she moved away from her father and stood a few feet from him, her eyes still downcast.

"She's a little shy," he explained in a low voice. "And she has to be exhausted. We've driven over eight hundred seventy miles in the past two days."

"Are you two hungry? I can make up some sandwiches." Abby bent a little and tried to catch the girl's eye. "Or a quick bedtime snack of ice cream and cookies?"

Joe studied his silent daughter with a pensive expression. "It's been a hard adjustment. Maybe after a good night's sleep…"

"Of course." Abby closed the door and slid the dead bolts home, then led the way upstairs. "I made up the daybed in your sitting room,'' she said in a hushed voice. ''I also brought in some extra towels.''

At Joe's room, Abby reached inside to flip the light switch and stood aside. The child hesitated in the doorway, her dark eyes wide as her gaze roamed over the rosebud-and-ivy-print wallpaper and lacy curtains.

''Pretty, isn't it?'' When the child shot a glance up at her, Abby gave her a conspiratorial grin. ''Not exactly a guy's room. Wait till you see *your* bedroom.''

Joe dropped the luggage just inside the door. The five-o'clock shadow on his face and his tousled hair, coupled with the sculpted muscles of his arms, gave him an almost threatening appearance—of someone who might be a street fighter, or a cowboy on the wrong side of the law—but his expression was gentle when he looked at his daughter. ''I'll be right back, Megan. I need to get a few more things from the car.''

The girl's uneasy gaze followed him until he disappeared down the stairs, then she took one faltering step onto the rose plush carpet of the bedroom. When the sound of Joe going out the front door filtered up the stairs, she stopped. Her lower lip trembled.

''Come on in, honey. I'll help you get settled,

okay?'' Abby crossed the room and turned on the light in the small half bath, then walked through the open French doors into the sitting room. White cotton curtains strewn with tiny rosebuds were gathered at the center of each door with a pink bow. ''You'll have plenty of privacy if you want to keep the doors closed and untie the ribbons.''

Megan gave a short, jerky nod.

''What do you think? This is a nice, sunny room during the day.'' The three large windows facing south and west were swathed in white eyelet curtains that matched the comforter and dust ruffle on the daybed. The rosebud-and-ivy wallpaper covered these walls, as well.

But even though this room would have been the stuff of dreams during Abby's childhood, Megan just silently scanned the area, then dropped her gaze to the tips of her shoes and swallowed hard.

Joe had claimed that he was gradually working his way across the country. Before abruptly taking off for Reno to pick up Megan, he'd vaguely referred to his divorce. No wonder the girl seemed upset—she probably hadn't seen her father for some time, and probably hadn't been too happy about leaving her mom behind, either.

''Tomorrow you'll get to meet the other people who live here,'' Abby said.

''Lindsey is just five, but she'll be so happy to

see another girl here. Maybe you two will be going to school together.''

For the first time, Megan lifted her stricken gaze to meet Abby's. ''I'm not *staying* here. I *can't*. I belong with Uncle Carl and Aunt Bonnie and my cousins.''

Taken aback, Abby searched for the right words. ''Well, Miss Coughlin,'' she said with a smile, ''I'm happy you'll be here for a little while.''

''My name is Graham. Megan *Graham*.''

''I see.'' But not really, and rising concern for this child's welfare made her probe further. ''So Joe isn't really your dad?''

''Yeah, but he didn't want me.''

Abby's heart stumbled. ''I'm sure he must love you, sweetheart.''

''Since I was four I lived with my mom or at Aunt Bonnie's house. He never came to visit me.''

''Oh, my.''

''He didn't even care when my stepdad adopted me.'' Megan's voice was almost inaudible. ''So my last name is different.''

A tangled history for such a little girl.

''Well, I don't imagine your dad means for you both to stay here very long,'' Abby said carefully. She reached out with one hand to the child, but Megan pulled back and wrapped her arms around her middle. "Won't it be nice to get to know him better?"

"No." Megan's eyes flicked toward the open doorway. "I'm *scared*," she whispered. "I wanna go *home*."

Everything that had driven Abby toward a career in social work now threw her senses into sharp focus as she dropped to one knee in front of the child and offered a hug with open arms. One word from this defenseless little girl and Abby was going to call 911, no further questions asked. "Tell me, sweetheart. Why are you afraid?"

Megan wavered, then backed up against a velvet padded window seat, her eyes wide. "He's got a *gun*."

Abby hadn't heard Joe come back up the stairs. Now she sensed him looming in the door behind her. Her heart skipped a beat.

"Not now I don't," he said heavily. "But I think we all need to talk."

CHAPTER FOUR

ONE LOOK AT the deep suspicion in Abby's eyes and Joe knew he needed to do damage control, and fast. He had no doubt that she'd be reaching for 911 at the slightest provocation. The irony bit deep.

There was nothing he wouldn't do to protect his daughter. Nothing he wouldn't do to keep her safe. Yet Abby and Megan were staring at him as if he were Jack the Ripper come to life.

"We're both a little overtired here," he said quietly from the door, without taking a step closer. "It's been a tough two days. Megan, did you tell her the reason I needed to bring you here?"

She shook her head.

"We lived in Colorado for a while, but after our divorce, my ex-wife remarried and took Megan to Texas. With both of them gone, I...left the area, too." He dropped his gaze to Megan's. "I missed you, sweetheart. Every single day."

The doubt on his daughter's face felt like a knife wound to his heart. When Abby moved behind

Megan and rested her hands on the child's shoulders in a gesture of support, that knife twisted.

"Why didn't you want me?" Megan whispered.

"You can't imagine how much I did." He expelled a long sigh, mentally cursing those who'd betrayed him and the court system that had refused to believe the truth. "But after your mom and stepdad died in that accident, I didn't have a good home for you. Your uncle and aunt did, though, with cousins to play with and a big yard. I was planning to come back in just a few more months."

"But Aunt Bonnie got s-sick." Megan's voice caught on a sob.

"She's getting the best possible treatment, honey. She'll be better in a few months, and you'll get to see her." He looked at Abby. "On the way here, a couple of bikers tried stealing my wallet. When they came after us, I had to take care of them."

Megan's lower lip trembled. "With a *gun*."

"It wasn't mine, sugar. It belonged to one of them. I gave it to the deputy when he took them away."

"How could you—unarmed—have managed that?" Abby said faintly.

"They were drunk, and probably high on something else, as well.'' Joe lifted a shoulder. ''Not quite as invincible as they thought.''

Actually, given their behavior and the supplies the deputy found in one of the biker's saddlebags, they'd probably been doing PCP. The deputy had returned from his cruiser's radio with the news that there were outstanding warrants on other drug charges, as well.

After questioning Joe and the teenage clerk in the gas station, the cops had cuffed and loaded the two guys into one of the cruisers and hauled them away.

''So you see,'' Joe added, turning his hands palm up in front of him, ''we were just in the wrong place at the wrong time—nothing more than that. Everything is okay.''

''Sounds like quite an adventure.'' Abby studied Joe for a long moment before her expression softened, though there was still a thread of steel in her voice. ''But you can understand my concern?''

Her concern could prove to be a problem if she nosed around too much or tried to interfere. And if she discovered what he was after, she could destroy evidence or disappear into the night.

But her concern warmed a small, frozen corner of his heart, as well. Where he'd been, no one had cared and there'd been more than a few who would have preferred him dead.

For far too long, he'd been surrounded by steel. Concrete. Lifers who'd sooner slide a knife between his ribs than say hello.

Just the sight of this woman, just the sweet scent of her, brought into painful focus all that he'd missed—all the business of living that had haunted his days and nights behind bars.

But though he'd yearned for freedom, he'd also long since accepted one immutable fact: there'd never be a day when he didn't remember the hell inside Coldwater, and he'd never again be the man he was.

Any naive faith he'd ever had in his fellow man had been destroyed the day he was sentenced, and he'd never be careless enough to trust anyone again.

ACCUSTOMED TO the soul-jarring clang of steel doors unlocking at four-thirty and breakfast by five, Joe was awake and restless long before the rest of the household stirred, his muscles tight and teeth clenched as he subconsciously awaited the familiar sounds that were no longer a part of his life. *Thank God.*

Back on Block 42, the others would be trudging through the wide gray corridors—surly, unshaven, silent, their eyes edgy and ever watchful as they headed for the grim, cavernous dining hall.

Early on, it had been easier to ID and avoid certain gangs by their ink—prison tattoos—but during the last year or so there'd been fewer who'd opted for such easy identification. Every passage to meals, every workout in the yard or weight room, had meant exposure and risk. Without his extensive DEA training in self-defense he would have been dead the first week.

On quiet, stocking feet he moved to the door of the sitting room and looked in on Megan. His heart turned over at the sight of her small, sleeping form beneath the quilt.

Dark eyelashes fanned against her rosy cheeks, and a tumble of dark curls framed her little face. In sleep she looked so innocent, so sweet, that his heart wrenched.

Given her wary distance, maybe they'd never have the kind of close father-daughter relationship Megan deserved. As much as he loved her, as much as he'd missed her, maybe she would be better off with the family who loved her, once Bonnie was back on her feet and in good health. Did he have the right to take her away from a good home—with two parents, and siblings, and a stable suburban life?

She stirred. Whimpered in her sleep and burrowed deeper into her covers. Was she dreaming of that incident back at the gas station?

He silently withdrew and headed down to the kitchen, where the boarders were welcome to start the coffeepot and make their own breakfast. During his first week here he hadn't bothered with more than a piece of toast and black coffee. Now he eyed the cast-iron skillet waiting on the stove and considered trying something more. Surely he hadn't forgotten how to—

"Hey, there. You're up early."

Startled at Abby's voice, he spun around, assessing the situation in a split second. She was in her stocking feet, too. Given her sweat suit and the Nikes dangling from one hand, she was planning to go running.

Forcing himself to relax, he managed a smile. "Always, I guess."

"You sure are jumpy. Believe me, I didn't think you were searching for heirloom silver." She moved to the refrigerator and withdrew a carton of eggs and a gallon jug of milk. "It wouldn't do you any good, anyway, because there isn't any."

He could think of a thousand questions to ask her, but right now her slender figure, nicely showcased as she searched a lower shelf for some other ingredient, seemed far more interesting.

She straightened and turned to meet his gaze with a wry expression in her own. "Want me to mix up some scrambled eggs for you before I go?"

He'd been here for six days before leaving to get Megan, and had figured delving into Abby's life would be easy during that first week. Instead, he'd found himself mowing the lawn and cleaning gutters, and had discovered that she was constantly gone. She left for school early and came home late, and there were times when she simply disappeared. Now, between a good breakfast and having some time with her alone, the decision was easy.

"Can I join you instead?"

She gave him a quick, sympathetic, head-to-toe glance. "Are you up to running? You still seem a little...pale."

"If I can't keep up, you can just leave me behind," he said dryly. "I won't mind."

"Megan?"

"She's still sleeping. I won't go for more than twenty minutes, and I'll leave her a note."

Abby pulled out a kitchen chair and sat down to put on her shoes. The amber and gold highlights in her curly hair shone under the lights overhead.

"That's all the time I have, anyway. I need to shower and leave for school by seven."

He leaned against the kitchen counter. "You sure run yourself ragged. Don't you take time for any fun? Even when you're here, it seems as if you're working nonstop."

"The semester ends next month. Term papers—

finals—I've got a few presentations to do—'' She blew her hair out of her eyes and pulled on her second shoe. "I'm carrying eighteen credits."

"So what's the rush?"

She shot an exasperated glance at him as she tied her laces. "A twenty-year-old doesn't have the responsibilities I do. I'm getting a late start at this thanks to—'' She cut herself short as she launched to her feet and started for the door. "Ready?"

Curious, Joe followed her onto the back porch and down the front steps.

"So...is this a second career?"

"You might say so," she muttered with a vague wave of her hand.

Maybe with dear Oren gone, she'd had to find other, more legal means of support. It was clear that she wasn't as well off as she'd been before.

"They say it's never too late to start over."

She snorted. "That's what I might say to my future clients, but I'm already thirty, and I need to make tracks. Speaking of which, we need to get started."

But the next time he could corral her into a conversation might be next week. He bent over to study his left shoe, then crouched down to untie the lace and readjust the tension. "Did I hear that you're going into social work?"

"Yes."

From the corner of his eye he discovered that she was tapping a toe.

"What's involved in that, exactly?"

He thought he could hear her grind her teeth. "I'll have my BSW by the end of summer session. After I start working, I'll begin taking classes for my master's. Look, I'm going to start out. If you want to catch up…"

"Nope. Let's go. It's too beautiful a day to waste, don't you think?"

A faint pink blush brightened the eastern sky over the rooftops of the old brick homes across the street and tinted the snowy Rockies to the west. The scents of damp earth and grass and hyacinths filled the air.

"Are you acclimated to the altitude yet?" Abby asked as she did her warm-up stretches on the concrete walk leading out to the street. "The mountains look far away, but we're a little over seven thousand feet. The air's a lot thinner than you might think."

Joe took a deep, appreciative breath as they started off down the street.

"It took a couple of days, but I'm fine." He nodded toward the funeral home next door, while carefully watching her expression. "Your place and that one look like a matched set. Are you in the funeral business, too?"

"Not directly, no. My brother-in-law is."

"Not directly?"

Ignoring his question, she picked up her speed. "Come on, or we'll be out of time."

Joe caught up easily and matched her pace. "I'm sorry about your husband's death last year." At her sharp glance in his direction, he added, "Sue mentioned him the other day."

"It was…certainly unexpected." Lengthening her stride, she pulled ahead as they passed the western edge of the town square. At Poplar she took a left and headed up into the hillier part of town. The stately homes gave way to a few blocks of smaller homes and finally to several blocks of 1950s ramblers.

Her stride faltered when a sleek black Mercedes appeared on a side street a block ahead. When the car turned toward them, she veered sharply up an alley without a word.

Joe followed her, but glanced over his shoulder a few seconds later. The car slid to a stop at the mouth of the alley. Through the lightly smoked glass, Joe could see the vague form of the driver leaning across the front seat to peer after her.

I'd give twenty bucks to see his expression, Joe thought grimly.

This was a town filled with ranch pickups and SUVs dusty from the wide-open country and gravel roads. The only black Mercedes he'd seen in town was the one at the funeral home, though the driver usually kept it in the attached garage and Joe had never seen his face. The guy had to be Abby's brother-in-law. But if so, why would she take such care to avoid him?

It was time to find out.

INVARIABLY, Joe's late wife had been a half hour behind with anything she did. Though he'd been in prison at the time, he'd heard that even her funeral started late.

Abby was gone by seven o'clock sharp, just as she'd planned, and how the woman could've showered, dressed and gone out the door so fast amazed him.

Abby had looked darn good, too—she'd stopped to ask him to fix a porch railing at the back of the house, and with just a touch of makeup her hazel eyes had sparkled beneath the graceful sweep of her long lashes. The healthy glow of her skin was undoubtedly due to good health and exercise, not some sort of potion or paint.

Sometimes, it was easy to forget—for just a heartbeat—about the reason he was here.

Joe had only to look into his daughter's face to remember.

''I've got Megan with me,'' Sue called out from

the entryway of the house. With slow, measured steps she herded Lindsey and Megan down the steps toward her gray Ford sedan in the driveway. "I hope she enjoys her first day of school."

Joe looked up from the forsythia bush he'd been trimming by the corner of the front porch. "I'd be happy to take the girls to school. I could save you a trip."

"As long as I'm able, I need to do for myself." Sue's voice sounded more breathless than usual, but she waved him away when he started toward her.

"I'm fine, really. It's just a short drive…and from there I'll be going…to the…library."

Another strong, independent woman, Joe thought grimly as he watched her wait for the girls to buckle their seat belts before she closed the passenger doors.

Until now he'd always thought those were purely positive attributes, but both Sue and Abby worked too hard, and Catherine, with her stiff pride and superior manner, probably had never even noticed the twinkle in Fred's eyes when he teased her.

"Bye, sugar," he called out to Megan. "I hope you find some new friends."

The almost imperceptible nod of her head might

have been acknowledgment…or simply a trick of the light through the window.

He could have followed them to the car and given her a hug goodbye, but he'd once tried to give her a quick, reassuring squeeze during the trip to Silver Springs and she'd moved aside faster than a startled fawn. The fact that she seemed to remember nothing of her first four years, when they'd been a family, hurt more than he'd ever want to admit.

Joe watched the Ford pull away from the curb, then set aside his hedge clippers and ran a hand through his hair. Ten minutes ago he'd seen the Mercedes pull out of the driveway leading to the back of the funeral home, but there'd been no other cars arriving or leaving since then.

The place wasn't all that busy, apparently, though given the size of this town that wasn't surprising. There'd been a glut of cars in the street a week ago for some funeral, but otherwise there'd been just a lawn crew parked in the circular driveway in front of the place every now and then.

Joe crossed Abby's grass and vaulted easily over the low brick wall separating the two properties. The difference between them was obvious the moment his feet touched the dense, lush lawn.

Abby's place was sliding into benign neglect, with overgrown shrubbery and myriad mainte-

nance projects begging for attention. Here, flower
beds already bloomed in bright, spring colors, and
there'd been attention to every detail—from the
crisp white paint on the fanciful gingerbread trim
along the eaves two and a half stories up, to the
freshly asphalted driveway and parking area.

He casually strolled around the brick building as
if simply admiring the landscaping. In back, he
found a formal entry with leaded-glass and oak
doors, offering mourners easy access from the
parking lot, while at the far end of the building
there were double garage doors. Across the parking
lot sat a four-stall brick garage flanked by rose gar-
dens just starting to bloom and a white lattice ga-
zebo.

"Hello, can I help you?"

Joe turned toward the building. A middle-aged
blond woman stood in the doorway, with one hand
on her slender hip and the other holding the door
open wide. The flattering cut of her beige suit and
her tasteful gold jewelry made him think of country clubs and old money, but the friendly, open
smile on her face dispelled any suggestion of ar-
rogance.

"I was just hoping to talk to the manager here,"
he said, sauntering toward her. "Is he around?"

"He's not available right now, but I'm Louise,

and I can help you get started. Would you like to come in?''

She ushered Joe down a wide hallway decorated in red-and-gold brocade wallpaper, and into a large reception area. At the other side, a high-arched doorway led to what was probably a visitation room.

The walls were covered with floral paintings set in massive, ornate gold frames. Dark mahogany chairs, small tables set with stained-glass lamps and silk flower arrangements seemed to fill every available space. Even the windows were over-whelming—covered in swaths of heavy lace, with heavy red brocade curtains tied back with gold tassels. The decor alone made the walls close in on him. The faint, museumlike mustiness in the air nearly robbed him of breath.

He could only wonder what jeans-clad ranchers thought of the place when they came to bid fare-well to their cronies. Perhaps, he mused, they con-sidered it a foretaste of hell.

''Would you like to sit down?'' she asked, ges-turing toward a discreet mahogany desk in the cor-ner. After he sat in the chair opposite hers, she studied him with carefully schooled sympathy in her eyes and pushed a box of tissues closer to him. ''You're the fella staying at Abby's place. You've lost someone close to you?''

"No—not at all. I've been doing some maintenance jobs for her, and I thought I'd stop over and see if there was any need for someone here."

Louise's expression cleared. "Well, I'm just delighted to hear that you don't need our services, Mr.—"

"Coughlin. Joe Coughlin." He settled back in his chair. "This is a beautiful place. Have you been here long?"

"Just a year or so. Mr. Hilliard has been here since the midseventies, of course. He's our director." Louise gave a modest dip of her head as she gestured around the room. "I do the silk- and fresh-flower arrangements here, and work part-time as his receptionist."

"You're very talented, Louise." When she beamed at him, he added regretfully, "It must take quite a crew of people to run a place like this—I suppose there isn't any chance that Mr. Hilliard would want extra help now and then."

"Really, I would think he might. We have lawn service and a local cleaning crew that comes in, but otherwise it's just Gene and me here. He brings in local guys to take care of maintenance jobs and sometimes it takes far too long to get anyone lined up." She pursed her lips. "With you just next door…"

At the sound of footsteps muted by the deep pile

carpeting, Joe looked up to see a man with thick glasses and thinning, pale brown hair enter the room. The buttons of his dark suit strained over the bulk of his midsection, and his tie seemed to be a tad too tight, if the florid color of his face was any clue.

"What have we here, Louise?" His voice held a hint of displeasure.

To her credit, she just gave him a bland smile. "You weren't available, and this gentleman had some questions. We were waiting for you to come in."

"There's a new floral order on your desk. Can you price it for me?"

Louise winked and waggled her fingertips at Joe—flirtatiously, if he wasn't mistaken—then sailed out of the room. When she was gone, Hilliard's fleshy features folded into a frown. "I've seen you around town," he said, crossing his arms across his chest.

"Probably."

"With my sister-in-law."

"I rent a room at her place."

"Something that's highly inappropriate. She certainly doesn't need to bring strangers into her home—especially men." Gene's eyes narrowed. "No matter how many times I tell her, she doesn't seem to understand. My brother would have been appalled.''

No wonder Abby tries to avoid the old prig. Joe forced a polite smile. "I'm only renting for a month or two. Actually, I came over to see if you needed help with maintenance. I could use a job while I'm in town."

"No. I'm sure there's nothing here…" Gene's voice trailed off as he moved to a window facing Abby's house and pulled a lace panel aside with a meaty hand. After a long pause, he turned to give Joe a calculating look. "Then again, maybe so. What can you do?"

"Basic maintenance. Some carpentry, a little electrical and plumbing. Lawn care. That sort of thing."

"Painting? Wallpapering?"

I will as soon as I check some books out of the local library. Joe nodded.

"Seven bucks an hour, no benefits, no guaranteed hours, on call?"

Bingo. The offer was lowball and the guy made Joe's skin crawl, but if the job gave him access to this place, he would have done it for free.

CHAPTER FIVE

LEAVING ONE SCHOOL and starting another so close to the end of the school year wasn't much fun, but leaving Uncle Carl and Aunt Bonnie was much, much worse.

Megan kicked a rock into the bushes behind Abby's house and dropped onto the grass. Across the low brick wall she could see into the yard next door, where Dad was on a ladder doing something to a second-story window of the funeral home.

She felt her cheeks warm, remembering the taunts of the kids at school. *"You live in that boardinghouse? What are you, poor or something?"* Even now, after three days, no one had been friendly. The teacher was pretty nice, but coming in six weeks before the end of school meant Megan had no idea about what was going on, and she sat silently at her desk most of the time.

There wasn't much to do here, either.

After school, Lindsey's mom came to pick her daughter up and take her to the library while she finished working for the day. Megan walked the two blocks home alone.

Dad had wanted to start coming to get her each day, but she'd cried and fussed until he finally gave in—though he still stood out along the sidewalk in front of the house and watched her every step of the way. If the other kids saw that, they'd think she was an even bigger loser. Though what did it matter? They were the losers, thinking that dumb things like the right clothes or shoes or backpacks mattered.

After the accident, nothing—not jeers or taunts or snubs—could ever hurt her as much.

Her eyes burned as she remembered the day long ago when everything had changed forever. The smell of squealing tires. The screams. The sounds of grinding metal and breaking glass, and the low moan from the front seat after the car finished rolling over and over and over.

Somehow she'd found herself out on the grass beside the road, surrounded by worried strangers who dabbed at the blood covering her arms and face and murmured words that she barely heard. She could still feel the hot sun, though. The stickiness. The grass prickling against her bare legs. The weird sense of not even being there—like it was all happening to someone on TV. Like it wasn't real.

If she closed her eyes, she could still see the car lying on its side like a crumpled toy. Her stepdad's limp, mangled arm hanging out of a shattered window. The dark wet pool on the cement beneath his fingertips.

The greatest horror had hit her when she realized that she hadn't been injured at all, and that the blood soaking her clothes wasn't her own.

She'd been only six years old, and the nightmares still came back.

Heaving a sigh, she rolled over onto her stomach and propped her chin against her upraised palms. From out on the street came the sounds of a girl's laughter and someone running. A second later, a golden retriever puppy romped around the corner of the house and made a beeline for her, his tail wagging furiously and his leash dragging.

Right behind him came one of the girls Megan had seen in the hallway at school, her blond pigtails flying, her bare, skinny legs pumping. Ashley? Aimee? Annie?

The puppy didn't even try to stop—he barreled into Megan, tipped her over onto her back, a fluffy, squirming, whimpering bundle of soft fur and pure excitement, his warm tongue tickling her ear. Laughing, she tried to wiggle free and then gave up and wrapped her arms around him and gave him a hug.

"Hey, I think Buffy likes you!" His owner flopped down on the grass next to Megan, grabbed the puppy's collar and hauled him over onto her own lap, where he twisted until he could reach up to lick her face. "We just got him a week ago and he doesn't have any manners yet. Are you the new girl? I'm Aimee Colwell."

Still a little breathless, Megan nodded as she sat up and dusted herself off. There were fresh green grass stains on her T-shirt now, and smudges all over from the puppy's damp paws, but she couldn't help grinning back at the freckle-faced girl next to her. "I'm Megan. Your puppy is sure cool."

Aimee ruffled Buffy's thick cloud of puppy fur. "He's not so good in the house yet. My dad gets *really* mad when Buffy pees on the floor." She rolled her eyes. "The puddle in the living room was the worst. We just got new carpet all over the whole house—light blue—and yesterday Buffy went right in the *middle* of the living room."

Back at Uncle Carl and Aunt Bonnie's, all the floors had been either hardwood or vinyl, and with four kids—plus her—and two dogs, there'd always been scuffs and footprints. "No sense in making life difficult," Carl always said. "Kids and dogs— that's what makes a good life. Not some fancy decorating." Of course, they hadn't had a lot of extra money for it, either.

Megan glanced at the boardinghouse, where she and Dad didn't own anything but the clothes they wore, and guessed that Aimee probably lived in a really nice house in the development a few blocks away, on the edge of town. "What did your parents say when they saw Buffy's accident?"

"World War Three." Aimee's mouth twitched as she scrunched up her freckled nose. "I...um... figured I could clean it up, so nobody would see. Do you *know*," she added dramatically, with one hand flung up to her throat, "what bleach will do to a carpet?"

Megan shook her head.

"Tell me—wouldn't you think bleach would *clean* it?"

"Well..."

"It did, all right." Aimee cupped the puppy's head with both hands and gave him a kiss on the nose, then laughed as he wriggled free and bounded back to Megan. "Took the blue color out, too. Ended up a yucky yellowy green."

For having faced such a disaster, Aimee didn't look too worried. "Weren't your mom and dad mad?"

"Yeah...but they always say things like, 'This is the last straw, young lady!' so I figure they won't stay mad very long." Aimee's grin slipped a little. "Dad said the puppy has to find a new home, but I don't think he means it. Hey, aren't you in Miss Darby's class? She's next door to Mr. Erickson, and that's where I am."

Stroking Buffy's powder-puff fur, Megan nodded.

"So we're both almost done with fourth grade. Maybe we'll see each other this summer. Do you swim? There's a pool across town."

"Well…I…" Megan shifted uncomfortably and folded her knees beneath her. Where *would* she be this summer? Here? Back in California?

Aimee's forehead furrowed as her gaze lifted to Abby's house, then landed back on Megan with a hint of sympathy. "But you're just sorta living here for a while, though. Like a hotel, right?"

"It's not like we're homeless, or anything," Megan retorted, feeling the warmth of embarrassment on her cheeks. Suddenly, it meant everything just to be accepted as an equal by this girl who lived here, in her own house, with a new puppy and parents who sounded as nice as Uncle Carl and Aunt Bonnie.

"We have a *big* house back in California. With lots of flowers and trees, and a white fence all around."

Aimee's eyes widened. "I didn't mean to…um…" Scrambling to her feet, she gathered up Buffy and started toward the street. "I...guess I better get home."

A little desperate now, her first chance at friendship slipping through her fingers like sand, Megan thought wildly for some way to make things better as she hurried to catch up. "I'm sorry. I didn't mean it, honest. It's just that..." She briefly closed her eyes and then plowed ahead, glad that no one else was around to hear. "My dad is a special kind of...of spy. He moves around a lot."

The lie came easier when Aimee stopped at the sidewalk in front and turned around. *"Really?"*

Megan nodded firmly. "But it's a secret—you can't tell. Okay?"

"Like, he carries a gun? And *shoots* people?"

Well, he'd had a gun back at the gas station on the way to Silver Springs...even if it hadn't been his. "He's really tough. I even saw him once—he beat up two big guys with his bare hands!"

"Cool!" Aimee breathed. "Like in the movies."

"Um...yeah."

"So what's he doing here?" Excitement sparked in Aimee's eyes as she gave a delicious shudder. "Did he follow some bad guys to Silver Springs? Oooh—maybe he's after someone who already lives here!"

The little white lie, only meant as a chance to

make a new friend, now felt like a rock the size of Texas in the pit of Megan's stomach. "You can't say a word. Promise," she said hurriedly.

"So it is! Who?"

"No—yes—I mean, I don't know. Honest. It's all secret. Or…or my dad could get hurt. And me, too."

Aimee gave her a conspiratorial grin. "Don't worry. My uncle's a deputy, and sometimes I overhear him talking to my mom about what he does. I never, ever tell—no matter how cool something is. Hey—I bet Uncle Rick would like to meet your dad!"

A distant, piercing whistle sounded. Buffy squirmed and whimpered, trying to get down to the sidewalk. "Oops—gotta go," Aimee said, looping the leash around her wrist. "That's my mom. See you at school, okay? I live just a few blocks away, so maybe we can walk together."

Megan nodded and managed a smile, but her insides still felt quivery and the lump in her throat made it impossible to say goodbye. Aimee's uncle was a *cop?* Dad was a drifter, not some superhero, and her story about him fighting and having guns had been a big mistake. Once she'd heard her cousin Logan whisper something about Dad being in a lot of trouble. What if she'd just made things worse?

Biting her lip, she retraced her steps to the back-yard. She braced her hands on the low dividing wall and hoisted herself up so she could sit and kick her heels idly against the sun-warmed brick. Dad was still over at the funeral home, on a ladder by the second-story window. It was partway open, now, and he was peering inside.

"Hey, Dad!"

He must not have heard her. Pushing the window sash higher, he glanced down toward the driveway curving around the building, and then climbed inside the building.

Frowning, Megan watched for him to come back out. Maybe he had to fix the window from both sides, she decided after a few minutes passed.

She shuddered, wondering what would be in there—imagining shadowy corners and weird smells and bodies. Did they just lie around on tables, waiting for a funeral? Sometimes there were noises and cars pulled up late at night, long after everyone at Abby's had gone to bed.

Living next door was a little creepy…yet she felt curious, too.

Surely it wouldn't matter if she got a little closer—just enough to take a quick look. She hopped off the wall into the other yard and cautiously crept up to the ladder. Tested the first rung. Wrapped her hands around the next one up.

A footstep crunched on the gravel behind her. "Young lady! *Where* do you think you're going?"

At the sound of the sharp male voice, she spun around in panic. Her sneakers, damp from the grass, slid sideways on the ribbed aluminum. She sprawled onto the ground, her pulse leaping and hands braced behind her—

And stared into the angry eyes of a man towering above her.

THE SECOND-STORY ROOM was some sort of an office-turned-storeroom, with drab gray walls, file cabinets and a cluttered desk adorned with a weedy-looking vine that trailed to the floor as if searching for water or a more hospitable home.

Joe surveyed the cardboard boxes stacked haphazardly in one corner. Old business records, maybe? Worth checking into—

From somewhere outside, Megan screamed.

Startled, adrenaline rushing through his veins, he flew to one side of the window and with the caution born of years in surveillance, he peered out, careful to avoid being seen from below.

Megan lay sprawled on the grass at the base of the ladder. Gene, his back to the window, stood over her, one hand jammed on his hip and the back of his neck bright red.

"You know this is trespassing. I could call the

police,'' Gene barked, shaking a finger at her, then pointing toward the street. ''Now, get out of here!''

Reining in a rush of protective parental anger, Joe grabbed his paint scraper from the floor and slid halfway out the window, calmly straddling the sill as if he'd been there for hours. ''Hey, honey, what's going on?'' he called out, his tone as casual as he could manage. ''Did you fall?''

Gene pivoted and craned his neck to look upward. His bushy eyebrows lifted in surprise, then lowered ominously. ''Where the hell were—what are you doing up there?''

Briefly lifting the scraper so Gene could see it, Joe eased the rest of the way out of the window and descended the ladder. ''Just doing what you asked—but the old paint is blistered, and these windows have to be scraped and primed again before painting.'' He hunkered down next to Megan, giving her a wink and a reassuring smile. ''Are you okay, honey?''

She cast a wary glance at Gene, then nodded.

''She was going up the ladder,'' Gene snapped. ''If this is your girl, you'd better keep a better eye on her.'' His eyes narrowed. ''Were you inside that room?''

Joe stood and helped Megan to her feet. ''Didn't know it was a problem. I needed a better angle for the highest panes. You do want the upper windows done, right?''

Pursing his fleshy lips, Gene studied him for a moment, then gave a stiff nod. His dark suit looked like fine wool—too warm for such a sunny spring day—and above the tight collar of his starched white shirt and tie, sweat glistened on his neck. ''All the trim, both floors.''

''Good, then. I ought to be done scraping in another day or so.'' Joe rested a hand on Megan's shoulder. ''Maybe you should head back to Abby's place, okay? I'll be home in an hour.''

Giving him a grateful look, she scampered across the property and disappeared over the brick wall. Beyond Abby's yard, a woman stood on her back porch, watching them. Joe tipped his head in her direction. ''Friend of yours?''

''Hmmph. A busybody, more like it.'' Gene adjusted his tie and straightened his lapels, then brushed an imaginary piece of lint from the breast pocket of his jacket. ''If you'll excuse me, I need to get inside. We've got a visitation starting in an hour.''

''Really. Must not be anyone important—I haven't seen a single florist truck arrive all afternoon.''

''Miffed'' wasn't a term Joe usually associated with male behavior, but it certainly fit the lifted chin and cold expression Gene shot in his direction. "Quint Galbraith, actually. One of the biggest ranchers in the area. And since you're working for me, you ought to know that we supply most of the floral arrangements in town. No matter what the occasion."

Joe tried to imagine wedding flowers arriving at a church via one of the vehicles emblazoned with Sheltering Pines funeral home on both sides. "You must be running a very successful business." He gestured toward the landscaped grounds in admiration. "No wonder you have such a beautiful place."

"Yes, well…" Gene glanced at his watch, then hurried toward the back entrance. "Perhaps you'd better stop for the day," he said as he opened the door and looked over his shoulder. "There will be cars arriving soon, and I'd rather not have workmen about."

"Sure. No problem. Hey—can I have a tour someday?"

Louise appeared in the doorway, beckoning urgently. "Phone call for you, Gene—line two."

She held the door for him, then lingered there with a faint smile and gave Joe a slow head-to-toe glance. "Stop in anytime when no one is around except me. Gene's a little touchy about tours—all those federal safety rules for OSHA, you know, with all the chemicals and so forth. But I'll be *real* glad to show you around.''

''Thanks,'' he managed to say, carefully ignoring the suggestive hint in her voice. He needed to get into the funeral home, but some prices were too high to pay. ''I'd appreciate that.''

He could feel her watching him as he turned to the ladder and released its hoisting rope, collapsing the extension section with a teeth-jarring screech of metal sliding against metal, and the hollow clang of the locking devices.

She was gone when he glanced back at the door.

CHAPTER SIX

"No, Mrs. Foley. I'm sure Joe is done for the afternoon and won't be bothering you anymore today." At the woman's sharp retort, Abby added firmly, "I'll make sure. Yes—I know the hammering must be disruptive."

With a deep sigh, she cradled the receiver and gave Joe a wry smile. "My neighbor is a bit..."

He glanced up from the garage-door opener he'd dismantled on the kitchen counter. "Difficult?"

Catherine, who was sitting at the kitchen table sipping Earl Grey and reading the *Silver Springs Gazette,* gave a ladylike sniff.

"Mildred Foley has been difficult since the day she was born."

"Catherine grew up here," Abby explained. "Anyone she didn't know as a child, she met while she was the town librarian."

Fred, who'd wandered into the kitchen a few minutes before, wearing his standard-issue Yankees cap and colorful suspenders, hoisted his coffee cup toward her in salute. "She remembers every last person who ever had an overdue book, too, and will hold it against 'em until the day they die.''

"Responsibility," Catherine retorted, "is a virtue not a vice."

"So what's the old biddy's problem this time?" Fred asked as he shuffled over to the oak trestle table by the windows overlooking the backyard.

"Hell's bells, a person can't hardly breathe and she's a callin'."

"Noise." Abby stifled a sigh. "Again."

"With that crazy nephew of hers, she's hardly one to throw stones. Ron says he's picked that boy up for speeding more times than you can count, and I heard he and those friends of his were running a—''

"There weren't any arrests," Abby interjected. "We don't know those rumors are true."

"But it don't take more than a good look at that boy to know he's trouble, pure and simple. And how many times has he been over here in the last month? Four—five times?"

"I don't think he would have come even once if he hadn't been sent." With the bloodshot eyes of someone who rarely saw dawn without a good hangover, Curt had been surly each time he appeared at Abby's door to complain about "the ungodly noise" or the errant wanderings of her dog.

He hadn't lingered long, though—after a litany of curses raw enough to blister paint and vague threats about "what's gonna happen if this don't stop," he always left abruptly. "This time Mrs. Foley was complaining about Joe working on the shutters. She says all the pounding has given her another migraine, and if the hammering continues, she will be calling the police."

"About someone putting in a good Saturday afternoon of work?" Fred drained his coffee cup and put it down on the counter with a thump. "I'd like to see the police department argue with that."

"Actually, if they were smart, they'd check their caller ID and hesitate to even answer when she calls in." Catherine rose stiffly and patted Joe on the shoulder as she made her way out of the room. "You go ahead, dear. Finish whatever it is you must do to those shutters, and ignore our little difficulty with Mildred." Her eyes gleamed. "Sometimes it's better to not give in."

A creed Catherine certainly lived by, though she did give in to a few of her own little vices. "Do you have a nice Saturday afternoon planned?" Abby called after her. "With your nieces?"

At the older woman's vague wave as she disappeared around the corner and into the hallway, Abby's heart sank. *Probably not the nieces, then.*

Catherine sometimes caught a bus coming

through town at three o'clock in the afternoon,
traveled over five hundred miles through the night
to a casino-filled town in Colorado, or to one of
the pari-mutuel tracks, and settled in for some fun
for a few days. She'd developed an alarming addiction to the greyhounds and horses, and to the
heady anticipation of dropping quarters in the slot
machines—never mind that she was on a tight
budget and faced mounting medical bills and in-
creasing disability with her advancing arthritis.

It had been a long time, though, since she'd
boarded that bus, and Abby had hoped the older
woman had quit for good. "I'm not her keeper,"
Abby muttered.

"What?" Joe snapped the cover back on the garage-door opener.

"N-nothing—" She faltered, caught for a moment by a sexy, sideways glance from those star-
tling eyes. "Just talking to myself."

A nosey landlady doesn't keep her boarders for
long, she reminded herself, and this one was wary
already. He'd hardly be thrilled to hear that she
was trying to save a grown woman from her un-
fortunate hobby.

"This ought to work for you now," he said,
eyeing her thoughtfully. "I'll go outside and give
it a test drive."

This afternoon, a faded Denver Broncos T-shirt

stretched taut over his biceps and chest. He'd lost his initial pallor, and given his dark hair and the amount of time he spent working outside at either Abby's place or the funeral home, his skin was already bronzed except for that narrow scar on his left cheekbone.

She'd noticed another scar, too—he'd been on the ladder, reaching to secure the top edge of a shutter, and she'd seen a scar on his side that had to be a good four inches long.

Wider than a surgical scar but straight as an arrow, the scar worried her. Had he been wounded in a fight? An unexpected attack? But when she'd mentioned it and expressed her sympathy, he'd brushed aside her concern with a nonchalant shrug and a change of subject, his voice flat and his eyes cold, and she knew she would never find out.

She wouldn't, because this footloose man wasn't her type, and he intended to move on in a few months. And after Oren, she had no plans to put her life in the hands of another man, ever. She reminded herself of that daily…because sometimes just an unexpected glimpse of Joe did strange, tingly things to her insides, and made her skin warm.

She followed him outside, where they stood in the driveway flanking the side of the house. When he touched the button on the opener in his hand, the garage door glided open.

"Super! This is going to be great the next time I come home in the pouring rain," she exclaimed, reaching over to give his arm a quick squeeze. The hard muscle of his forearm jerked beneath her fingertips, sending a tremor of sensation dancing up her arm, and she quickly took a step back. "Thanks."

"No problem."

From the bushes on the side of the garage came the sound of giggling. Hamlet ambled into view, his long ears dragging on the ground, followed by a puppy trying to pounce on them. Lindsey, Megan and Aimee emerged from the bushes a moment later, and ran laughing around the opposite side of the house, the dogs in fast pursuit.

"I think your little girl has made a new friend."

The laugh lines at the corners of Joe's eyes deepened. "I'm not sure your basset is all that thrilled."

"Megan seems to be adapting," Abby ventured, watching Joe's expression. Today was the first time she'd seen the child appear so carefree—but even so, Abby still detected a hint of haunting loneliness in Megan's eyes. *No wonder, given all she's gone through.* "How about you?"

Joe's gaze cut to hers. "Adapting?"

"To parenting. Since…um…it's been a while."

He gave a curt nod. "Fine."

She waited, letting the silence lengthen between them, but he didn't elaborate. If she hadn't been watching him so closely, she wouldn't have seen a tense muscle twitch at the side of his jaw.

He worked hard, he didn't complain, and he was good to his daughter. If he had secrets, he certainly held them tight. "Um…well, then…I guess I'd better get back to my homework. Thanks for fixing the door."

"Anytime." He bent to pick up his toolbox, the muscles of his back flexing and bunching beneath his thin T-shirt, then he strode toward the garage like a man taking charge and getting things done.

Not, she mused, like a drifter who couldn't keep a job. But if he wasn't the man he claimed to be, why was he living in a boardinghouse, in the middle of Nowhere, Wyoming?

IF SHE HADN'T been tossing and turning, unable to sleep, she might not have heard the noise outside.

A whisper.

The rustle of the lilac bush along the driveway that skirted the house beneath her window. Hushed voices out by the garage.

Sitting up in bed, she stilled, her heart thumping. Throwing back the covers, she hurried to the small eyebrow window under the eaves. Standing on the brocade settee beneath the window, she peered out into the darkness.

At the soft rap on her door, she started, one hand at her throat. No one ever came up the steep, narrow steps to her rooms, even during the day.

"It's me." Joe's voice was, an almost intimate whisper that none of the others would hear. "Are you awake?"

"Is something wrong?"

"There's someone outside, near the garage. Is there anyone you'd expect to be out there at this time of night?"

Abby shot a worried glance at the digital alarm clock by her bed. "Not at *midnight*." From outside came the faint crash of glass falling against concrete. "I thought I locked the garage, but—"

"I'll check it out."

"No, wait. I'll call the pol—"

"*No.* Just stay put."

Before she could answer, she heard his light footsteps race down the stairs to the second floor. And a few moments later, the soft creak of the front door.

The room suddenly felt much colder. Shivering, she pulled on her heavy fleece robe and eyed the telephone on the bedside table. He'd sounded so adamant, yet what if there was a burglar out there? Someone who could overpower him—maybe even hurt him? *I should call 911, anyway.* With shaking fingers she dialed and gave the details.

Outside, something crashed into the bushes. She heard a yelp, then raised voices hushed by one much deeper. One that was in absolute control.

Joe.

Dropping the phone, she flung open her bedroom door and hurried down the two flights of stairs as quietly as she could, crossed the kitchen and flipped on the backyard lights.

Maybe, she realized as she stepped onto the porch, she should have followed orders, because he was in no trouble at all. The two lanky teenagers were, though, from the stark expressions on their pale faces and the awkward bend of their arms where he held each one at the crook of the elbow.

Even if they were vandals, she couldn't help but feel a touch of compassion. "What's going on out here?"

"Well?" Joe growled at the two boys. Lit by the security light over the garage, he appeared lean and menacing, his dark hair tousled and too long, his five-o'clock shadow and the glitter in his eyes suggesting that he was well capable of taking care of any young punks who crossed his path.

The shorter one darted a cautious glance at Joe, then gave her a beseeching look. "Nothin'. Me and Jase were—"

"Give me a break," Joe snarled. "Starting by telling me your name."

The boys probably sixteen or seventeen, dropped the plaintive expression and set his chin at a surly angle. He tried to jerk away, but Joe hauled him back to stand next to his buddy.

"Jeez, man. We were just foolin' around. Didn't mean anything."

"Your *name*."

The boy looked left and right for an escape route, but Joe still held his arm. After a long moment, he muttered, "Sam."

"Breaking and entering isn't just fooling around, Sam. Trespassing. Property damage. Maybe you'd like to tell the lady what you did to her car?"

The taller boy—Jason, apparently—shuffled his feet. "I…we…sorta broke the side mirror."

"And?"

Jason glared at Abby. "A can of paint fell off the shelf, okay? No big deal. It'll probably come off with paint remover, or something."

"Oh," Abby said faintly, remembering the child's wooden rocker she'd stripped and repainted out in the garage a few weeks ago, as a present for an old friend. "Not the pink."

Joe lifted an eyebrow. "Nice contrast, on your red Chevy."

He released the two boys, but from the coiled tension in his body it was clear that he was ready to go after them if they tried to take off. "Now we have to figure out what these gentlemen owe you."

Sam shifted his feet. "Hey, man…"

"Let's see. The lock on the side door of the garage was broken. The hinges are bent. There's the replacement of the mirror, and possibly some bodywork if the door was weakened there. Sand-blasting and painting the car. Anything else?"

"I got the money, but I'm sure not—"

"Yes, you are." He gave them both a disdainful look, then tipped his head and stilled, listening. From down the street came the sound of an approaching car. "Did you call the police, Abby?"

"I was worried—I didn't know who was out here, and thought I'd better."

"Well, then, you boys now have a choice. Deal with me, or deal with the law. I'd guess," he added, "that you two have quite the history around town. How old are you?"

Jason's mouth curled into a sneer. "Eighteen."

"Adult court, then. Bad news."

Sam punched his brother's arm. "C'mon, you know what that cop said last time."

A vehicle pulled to a stop in front of the house and a car door slammed.

"This is the deal," Joe said quietly. "We let

that officer take you two in, we press charges, we sue for damages. This will be in the newspapers. Having a record will hurt you with job applications, with college financial aid, and anything else you want to do. Or, you can repay all the damages, and starting Monday you can come over to help Abby around this place for…say, twenty hours apiece as an apology.''

''What?'' Jason's expression was incredulous.

''And, you'll be polite. Friendly. Personable. On time. You can consider it a work-release program from the jail you don't have to be in. And you can bet that I will hunt you down if you ever fail to show up. Clear?'' He nodded toward the cell phone clipped to the older boy's back pocket. ''Now call your dad so we can discuss this.''

''No!''

''You don't have a choice. He'll be easy enough to find—and if I have to do that, I'm not going to be happy. Got it? Now, dial. Explain this fast and then give the phone to me.''

After what was apparently a heated argument with his father, Jason handed the phone to Joe, just as footsteps crunched up the driveway.

A tall officer dressed in a navy blue uniform and a fully loaded service belt strode into view—Rick Colwell, Abby realized, as he moved into the dim pool of illumination under the security light.

Joe eased away from the light, his thumbs jammed into the back pockets of his jeans and his expression grim as he continued to talk on the phone.

Rick nodded toward Abby and Joe, then surveyed the two boys, his forehead furrowed. "Sam. Jason. A little late for the Cailey brothers to be out on the street. Isn't it?"

The teenagers studied the toes of their shoes.

Rick pulled a small spiral notebook and pen from the breast pocket of his uniform. "Damages?"

"We were…um…just discussing how this could be handled." Abby glanced at Joe, then plowed ahead. "Boys? What will it be?"

"You," Sam mumbled.

Jason's shoulders slumped with apparent relief. "Goes for me, too."

"You're sure? You're making a commitment, and you have to follow through. I imagine I can always call Rick back if there's any problem."

His arms folded across his chest and his stance wide, Rick studied Joe, then Abby. "Exactly what's going on here?"

When Joe didn't speak up, Abby gave a little shrug. "The boys were trespassing, and caused some damage. They've decided to pay for the repairs, and we'll let it go at that."

Rick snorted. "It would be better if you pressed charges and let me haul them in. Daddy pays, they get off, and there's no lesson in that."

"They'll be coming back to work some of it off."

Rick's eyebrows rose. "Good luck. Then again," he added, "maybe your friend can make it work. I hear Joe's quite the guy."

From the corner of her eye, she saw Joe stiffen. "I'm not sure what you mean."

The radio mike on Rick's shoulder crackled, then gave a burst of static. When he touched a button, a dispatcher rattled off a series of codes and an address north of town. "Gotta go," he said. "Sounds like you're all set here—even if your plan isn't a good idea. Call me if things change."

"Thanks."

"Oh—and tell your friend that he and I ought to have a real nice talk sometime. Sounds like we might have a few things to discuss."

Abby stared after him as he rounded the corner of the house and disappeared. She had school to finish, boarders to take care of, a difficult brother-in-law to deal with. And now, two young vandals and a boarder who grew more mysterious by the moment.

What on earth had Rick meant?

GENE RUBBED a hand through his hair, belatedly remembering the precise arrangement of the longer strands that he so carefully combed over the gleaming top of his head every morning and sprayed with Super Hold Hair Spray.

Grimacing in disgust at the tackiness of the spray against his damp palm, he reached for his cup of amaretto-flavored coffee and savored a long swallow before turning back to the papers on his desk. He shuffled through them, then shoved them aside.

It had been so much easier when Oren was alive.

In the old days, Oren had been the business manager and director of all four Sheltering Pines funeral homes. He'd taken care of ordering, inventory records, insurance and billing at the main office in Dalton, handled auditors and inspectors and the IRS, and left Gene to enjoy what he did best—artistic presentation of the deceased, whatever the cause of death. Placating widows and dealing smoothly with shell-shocked widowers who wanted only the finest send-off for their beloved—if not out of love, then out of guilt.

There hadn't been much time to prepare for his new management role—one day Oren was at the helm and as controlling as ever, and the next, he was laid out on a slab after suffering a massive heart attack. Which just went to show that it wasn't only the good who died young.

"Had it all, you bastard," Gene muttered to the oil painting of Oren and Abby that still hung on the wall of his office. The ornate gold frame sparkled through its heavy layer of dust. "Money. Country club. A beautiful wife, and you sure as hell let me know about it often enough. But where'd it get you?" He allowed himself a small, satisfied smile. "Six feet under."

It was reassuring to know that there was justice, if one waited long enough. And, Gene conceded, it was also quite helpful having the example of Oren's mistakes to guide him. No one, except some anonymous lab tech in Cody and the county coroner, knew the *exact* cause of Oren's death, but the man's last, foolish mistake had been the best lesson of all.

At a light tap on the door, Gene jerked his thoughts back to the present.

"Yes?"

"Just me," Louise purred. "Did you want me to go after something for lunch? I can run over to Charlie's for you—the Wednesday special?"

"Ah...no. A club sandwich, skip the mayo... raspberry tea..." He paused, rationalizing away the impact of a few extra calories. "And the cherry-swirl cheesecake, if they have it."

"Back in a few minutes," she called out as her footsteps retreated down the hall.

Shifting his weight, Gene reached for the files and thumbed through them until he found the one holding his newest roster of suppliers. The memory of that last threatening phone call gave him a shiver of unease, but he quickly brushed it aside. As always, he'd be careful.

A warm feeling of satisfaction eased through him when he heard the front door open and close. Louise liked him, he could tell. She wanted to please him. Women always went for men with money and power, and now he had it all in spades.

If he handled things right, he could retire early, marry a looker like Louise—but someone much younger, of course—and live a life of ease.

CHAPTER SEVEN

ABBY STARED OUT over the backyard in amazement. The late-Friday-afternoon sun turned the side of the garage golden, and the neatly clipped lawn was a deep, fresh emerald, with that wonderful lush appearance only seen in this part of Wyoming with ample watering in the spring. The riotous, rainbow-hued petunia beds rimming the garage and house—Lindsey's choice of colors—were neatly weeded.

Joe stood leaning a shoulder against the corner of the garage, his muscular forearms folded across his chest, as Sam and Jason picked up the garden tools and then looked up at her expectantly.

"This okay?" Sam asked.

Joe glanced in his direction. *"Ma'am."*

"Ma'am." Sam repeated. He jerked a shoulder in silent rebellion, but she could see a faint hint of pride in his face over the good job he'd done. For someone with three silver rings in one ear, piercings through both eyebrows and an obvious propensity for breaking the law, he was actually a pretty decent kid to have around.

"Wonderful," she called out. "Everything looks absolutely wonderful."

Joe checked his watch. "Go on then, guys. See you next week, right after school. And after you get done with your hours here, I want to hear how you're coming with some job applications for the summer."

After they took off on their mountain bikes, Joe sauntered over to the porch steps, resting a foot on the bottom step and his elbow on the railing.

"Heard anything more from their parents?"

"Nope. I thought I would, since Mr. Cailey was so huffy with you during that first phone call."

"Huffy?"

She chuckled. "All I heard was your side of the conversation, but I saw your knuckles go white while you were gripping Jason's cell phone."

"Cailey's wife was in the background, and she didn't sound pleased. I think she helped change his thinking a little—I heard her tell him at least three times that repayment had to be better than footing the bills for lawyer fees and court appearances." Joe snorted. "Sam says his dad is quite a golfer. If Cailey spent more time with those two boys and less time at his club, this situation might not have come up in the first place."

She'd thought of Joe as an irresponsible wanderer—a deadbeat dad with little concern for his own child, much less anyone else's. But during this past week, she'd often found herself at the window when she got home from school, watching him work alongside the two teenagers. He talked easily with them. Joked. She'd seen him ruffle Sam's hair and give Jason a brotherly clap on the back for a job well done.

From the very start, something had sparked between Joe and her—she felt it every time their eyes happened to meet—but she'd tried to ignore it. Attraction was one thing, acting on it was another, and she was too experienced to head down any paths leading toward a foolish mistake. Her youthful infatuation with Oren had been lesson enough on *that* score.

She just wished she could get past Joe's wall of reserve and find out more about him. Why hadn't he settled down, found a house, a wife, a regular job? But every time she tried to delve into his past, he slipped away as skillfully as a wild buck, evaded her questions and disappeared.

Sure she could somehow help him get his life back on track, she was going to try again tonight.

"So," she remarked, as she surveyed the white wrought-iron chairs and table out by the petunias, "I don't suppose you're going out to the elementary school tonight? For the open house?"

"The what?"

"Lindsey put her note up on the refrigerator. Didn't Megan give you hers?"

"No…she didn't."

"Well, it's at seven o'clock, and I'd be happy to come with you since you're so new in town. The kids have projects set up in the rooms, and the teachers will be there to talk to the parents."

"She's just been here two weeks, though."

"All the more reason to see how she's doing with her classmates and teacher, don't you think?"

"Of course." His eyes took on a faraway expression, and Abby wondered what he was thinking. "I'd like the chance to do this," he said finally. "I've missed out on too much already."

IT SEEMED like something out of a black-and-white TV rerun, walking down the street on this balmy, small-town evening, with Abby beside him and Megan trailing behind.

The houses in this part of town were all old-money solid, four-square, with full-length front porches painted white and pretty hanging flower baskets. Neatly trimmed hedges and long flower beds dividing one manicured lawn from the next. There were other, less affluent areas of town—the trailer court, the dusty little clapboard houses whose yards were littered with sun-faded toys and the rusting hulks of an old pickup or two.

But here—free to walk down Oak with his daughter and Abby—he imagined what his life might have been if he'd caught his suspects back in '99, had never been set up and had never seen the inside of those prison walls. He might have owned a nice house. Had a few more kids. Moved up in the DEA.

"Hey," Abby said, bumping his arm with her elbow. "You look awfully grim. Going to an open house really isn't that bad."

Bad? These ordinary family activities were what he'd dreamed of, what he'd never expected to experience. Megan would have been in her mid-twenties and he would have been in his fifties at the end of his full sentence. "I think I'll survive," he said dryly. "Have any pointers?"

"Be nice to the moms. Respectful of the teachers. And—" Abby shot a mischievous glance at him "—compliment the PTA ladies on their coffee and cookies."

He turned partway and extended a hand to Megan, but she just slowed and fell back another few feet. "How about you, honey? Have any advice for your dad?"

"No." She studied the sidewalk as she walked, her face somber. "Just that it's stupid to go. Maybe we could just go to the park instead?"

She had his wavy black hair and light blue eyes,

but had inherited her mother's delicate features and already showed signs of becoming a beauty when she grew up. Right now, though, that stubborn set to her jaw reminded him all too much of his former mother-in-law. "Another time. This is important, Megan."

"No one even knows me here. Not really, and we'll be gone before next fall, anyway." At the steps of the school a few minutes later, her voice took on a pleading note. "I did better at school before I came here, honest. Uncle Carl helped me with math and Aunt Bonnie checked my papers...everything was always okay then."

Her words stung, even as they hit home. He asked her every day about school, and she always mumbled "fine." He hadn't realized that she might need help. Another way in which he was failing as a father.

"I just want to be a part of your life again, Megan," he said as he held open the door and ushered her and Abby through. "We can make this a quick visit and then go, okay? And when you need any help with something, I'll do whatever I can."

Inside, they stepped into a swirling melee of color and noise, of jostling elbows and kids darting this way and that.

Abby touched his arm. "I'll run over to Lindsey's class for a minute, then I'll find you,'' she said over the din.

Megan trudged through the crowd to room 104, where a cluster of bright red helium-filled balloons bobbed wildly above the door. Her shoulders sagged as she mumbled a greeting to the perky young thing—he wondered how someone who looked seventeen could be a *teacher*—standing just inside the door.

Joe first sensed something wrong when Miss Darby's cheerful smile faltered as he shook her hand.

"I'm glad you could come tonight," she said, her gaze already sliding to the next set of parents coming through the door. "Megan can show you around."

The room was as bright as a carnival, with colorful construction-paper collages on the walls, papier-mâché creations on a table by the windows and bookcases overflowing with books along the inner wall. Parents hovered at their children's desks, admiring papers and test scores, while younger siblings examined what appeared to be science projects on the long counter at the back or wandered through the room. Several were at the blackboard drawing pictures.

"My desk is over here now," Megan murmured, stopping at the front row. She opened the manila folder lying on her desk. "I don't have much to show."

Resting a hand on her shoulder, he reached down to lift up one paper, then another, complimenting her on each one. Most of them—from science tests to math to social studies—showed an awful lot of red ink, though a poem boasted a "Good Job!" at the top.

He realized with a sudden pang, that he had no idea how well she'd done in school up until now. Did she struggle to learn? Did she need extra help?

"Can we go now?" Megan pleaded, glancing uneasily at the other families in the room. *"Please?"*

"In just a minute." He looked up then, and realized that some of the kids were whispering and some of the parents were looking cautiously in his direction. And Megan's cheeks were bright pink. "Maybe," he said, bending down to speak close to her ear, "you want to tell me what's going on?"

"They all grew up here. We're new."

"That's it?"

"That makes me *different*. I shouldn't have even come here!"

Miss Darby was moving through the room now, speaking to parents, praising school projects. She must have heard Megan, for she suddenly changed course and came up to the front row. "Your daughter is a delight,'' she said, smiling down at Megan. ''Such a sweet girl.'' The warmth in her expression faded when she looked up at Joe. ''We usually don't have our end-of-the-year school conferences until late May, but I wonder...could you and I talk sometime soon?''

At Megan's sound of distress, Miss Darby rested a hand on her shoulder blades. ''Just because you're new, sweetie. We always...um...like to get to know the parents.''

''Name the time.''

''Monday—at three-thirty?''

''I'll be here.''

Megan gave him an accusing glare, then started for the door.

''Wait.'' The teacher thumbed through Megan's papers, then handed him the poem. ''Take this,'' she whispered. ''Read it before you come in. I'd suggest you not discuss it with your daughter, though. Not yet.''

He felt the stares of the parents when he folded the paper and put it in his pocket, then left the room. Small towns could be insular places, where newcomers weren't welcome, but he sensed something far more than simple curiosity.

And hoped like hell that no one knew why he was really here.

LONG AFTER MEGAN went to sleep that night, Joe sat on the swing on Abby's front porch with the lights off. Crickets sang from the bushes. The heady scents of damp grass and lilacs, and a hint of faraway pine, filled the air. With the tall shrubbery at either side of the porch, it was a perfect place to be alone with his thoughts.

Megan's free-verse poem still lay on his lap, childish and awkward in form, but each word had burned like acid into his heart.

> Why did my mother have to die?
> She was the sun in my life, the parent who stayed,
> She was the one who loved me.
> The one who laughed, and had fun,
> The one who should have lived forever.
> Now I have no one, no one who cares.
> Why did things have to end up so wrong?

He'd thought she was adjusting fairly well—she went to school and hadn't complained very often, she played with Lindsey and the girl from her school. She ate as well as he supposed a child should eat, and seemed to sleep okay. But what the hell did he really know about raising a child?

The day he'd agreed to give Sheri full custody, he'd thought he was doing the right thing. With his undercover work, he'd sometimes spent weeks in the field, and he knew a four-year-old needed a far more stable home than he could provide. Sure, he'd visited often, taking Megan for weekends whenever he could, but that sure hadn't prepared him for full responsibility now.

Lost in thought, he barely heard a car easing to a stop out on the street, until he glanced up and noticed that its headlights were off.

The interior lights flicked on for a few seconds. Across the stretch of front lawn he couldn't make out the driver's features, but the guy appeared to be studying something in his hand.

Curious now, Joe launched to his feet and stood at the corner of the porch where the shrubbery would conceal him.

A moment later, the car rolled forward...and turned quietly into the driveway of the Sheltering Pines. *Bingo*. The relatives of someone newly deceased wouldn't be likely to drive with their headlights off. Turning on his heel, he crossed the porch and started down the front steps.

The screen door behind him opened. ''Hey, what's up?''

Startled at the sound of Abby's sleepy voice, he nearly lost his footing. *Damn*. He turned to find her in her fuzzy pink robe cinched tight at the waist and held at the top with one hand, her curly hair tousled and her eyes filled with concern. "I couldn't sleep."

She eyed his running shoes and jeans, then her gaze darted past his bare chest. "You were going running, at this hour?"

"No…just sitting out here, thinking about Megan. Then a second ago, I thought I saw something suspicious—a prowler, maybe."

"Not *again.*" She gave a watery laugh. "Believe me, I've lived here for a year, and until those two boys dropped in last week, I would have felt safe leaving a silver tea service on the front lawn."

He watched her expression carefully. "It was a car this time. It slowed down in front of your house, then it pulled into the driveway next door."

"The funeral home? It doesn't exactly have nine-to-five hours."

"The car didn't have its headlights on."

"If that was someone who lives in town, they might not think to turn on their lights…and the street lamps would light the way."

Either she believed it was nothing more than routine business, or she was one of the best liars Joe had ever met.

He wanted to vault over the porch railing and check out that car—to get a look at the license number, and see who could be dropping in after midnight. He'd been watching Abby for a couple of weeks now, casually trying to ferret out information, and hadn't made any significant progress. To his frustration, he hadn't yet gotten access to any files over at the Sheltering Pines, either, because Gene was nearly always there.

But now, with Abby at his heels, he could hardly risk raising any questions about his own motives for being here. Stifling a sigh, he kept an eye on the street and gave a little shrug. "Guess I'm overly cautious."

"Not a bad thing, really."

A shadowy car pulled out of the driveway next door, and headed up the street in the opposite direction—taillights off. He swore softly under his breath.

She gave him a curious look. "What?"

"Nothing…just thinking." But the car was gone, the opportunity missed, and Abby didn't look as if she was planning to go back into the house anytime soon.

Which maybe wasn't such a bad thing after all. He'd finally seen some suspicious, late-night activity—his first real break—so it could happen again. And if anyone had noticed him on the porch they might have seen Abby, too—just two ordinary people up late at night, nothing more.

She moved to the railing a few feet away and inhaled deeply, the corners of her mouth tipped up in appreciation. ''Isn't it beautiful out here at night?''

''Yes, it is.'' And now that he could give her his full attention, the most beautiful thing he could see was her. Her pale, creamy skin glowed in the moonlight, her long, dark lashes shadowed her cheeks. Even with that bulky robe, her slender curves were clearly in all the right places.

''I'm sorry I didn't find you and Megan at school—when I finally made it to Miss Darby's class, you were gone.''

''No problem.''

''I had to go see Lindsey's projects, and then she wanted to show me everything in the room. I think,'' she added with a dry laugh, ''that I had the most complete tour on record. Sue was there, too, but she was too tired to do more than rest and look at Lindsey's school papers. By the end of the day, she's just exhausted.''

He'd come to town assuming that Abby knew about her late husband's little business on the side, and figuring that she'd even taken an active part. It wasn't easy to launder significant sums of money through a small business in a small town, so it was likely that she'd helped juggle the books, at the very least. But the more he saw of her compassion for everyone around her, the less he thought that could have been true.

And, unfortunately, the more he saw of her, the more intriguing she seemed.

Maybe he wasn't DEA any longer, but even an ex-agent knew the risk of falling for a suspect. It clouded vision, put the entire investigation at risk. And this was one investigation that couldn't fail if he was ever to clear his name.

"What will happen to her?" he asked.

"Sue? She's hoping to move into her own subsidized apartment at the end of the month. It will be better than here—on a ground floor, with handicapped facilities if she ends up in a wheelchair. It's close to the library and Lindsey's school, too."

"And then you'll have to try finding another boarder?"

Abby bit her lower lip. "Maybe—but it would only be short term."

"Ah…you're going to marry that deputy who hangs around and live happily-ever-after in this house?"

"Marry Rick? No. He stops by now and then but we're just friends. I've been single, married and widowed, and I think single is best by far." Abby lifted an eyebrow. "How about you?"

He hadn't been with a woman in so long, he couldn't even remember how good it felt. But he did remember the last throes of his marriage, and that hadn't been good at all. "I'd rather travel light."

"Marriage isn't always what you expect," she said, giving him a weak smile.

"A few disappointments build into major problems, the attraction goes, and you're just left with pieces of the dream. The irony is that I've thought about going into counseling as a career, and here I've been a failure myself."

"Not a failure—you've had experience, and you can empathize. Some relationships never should have started in the first place."

She laughed aloud at that. "Tell me about it."

It was a chance to get more information about Oren Hilliard, but suddenly he found he was even more concerned about what this gentle, caring woman had gone through. "What happened?"

"Chalk it up to naïveté, a desperate mother and economics." Abby wrapped her arms around her middle and paced to the corner of the porch, then back again. "We were poor, my dad split when I was twelve, and my mom had four girls to launch into the world. College wasn't an option out of high school. It was the local packing plant or early marriage, so when I caught Oren's eye…"

"Let me guess. He was older, successful, and liked his women young?"

"You nailed it. He drove up one day in his shiny Cadillac, and Mom almost kissed his feet. She wanted us girls to have the secure home and money that she never had, so she wasn't interested in matters of the heart, especially when he promised to help pay off her bills.''

Disgust rose like bile in Joe's throat at the thought of a middle-aged man lusting after a young girl. ''She essentially sold you off.''

''Oh, I could have refused and just gone off on my own, but I had three younger sisters to think about, and I'd just turned eighteen. I didn't have any skills, didn't know where to go. And Oren sure knew how to promise the moon.'' She shook her head. ''I even convinced myself that I loved him.''

''So…how did it all work out?''

''Let's just say I'm not the poster child for happily-ever-afters.''

''That bad?''

''No. He lost interest after a couple of years, and we sort of led separate lives after that. I did a lot of volunteer work and was able to help my sisters through school, and then my mom's health grew worse…'' She turned away and looked up at the stars. ''He was Catholic, so he didn't believe in divorce, and he had what he wanted—a wife, stability. I was able to help a lot of people. A good trade-off, don't you think?''

Joe felt like shaking her, and asking how she could have given up so much.

''You couldn't have just found a way to leave?''

''I was on the verge, but then he died…

suddenly. He'd never even had any heart trouble before then.''

Even before he asked his next question, he felt like a traitor. "So…did you work with him in the business?''

"Some.''

"Doing what?''

Her eyes took on a knowing look, as if she'd faced frank curiosity from the public all too many times, and had wearied of answering. "Did I embalm anyone? Of course not.'' She glanced at her watch. "Good heavens, it's already after one o'clock. I don't know about you, but I need to get some sleep.''

In a flash she was gone, leaving just the faint scent of roses in her wake.

Joe stared after her, then turned back to brace his hands on the porch railing and stare out into the night.

Abby was hardly the brittle socialite he'd expected. She'd sacrificed, and she'd suffered to help her family. She'd honored her vows when most women would have cut and run. The big question was just how much she'd helped Oren, but even that possibility couldn't stop the quiet warmth that now settled around Joe's heart.

CHAPTER EIGHT

HE MIGHT HAVE MISSED checking out that suspicious car last night, but Joe didn't plan on missing his next opportunity.

It came at eight o'clock on Monday morning, with a phone call from Louise about a leaky faucet in the public rest room at the funeral home. He arrived as soon as Megan left for school.

"Thanks for coming so soon," Louise trilled as he walked in the front door.

"That drip-drip-dripping is driving me insane."

It had been years since he'd had to do even the most minor plumbing, so he'd checked out his well-thumbed *Homeowner's Weekend Guide* for the basic instructions, and then crossed his fingers.

Sure enough, it proved to be a simple matter of using the washers in a five-dollar faucet-repair kit, rather than replacing the entire faucet. Still, he dawdled and examined and tinkered until Louise finally grew bored and disappeared.

After that, it took less than five minutes to finish the job and five more to pack up his tools. He left them in the bathroom, then wandered through the main floor of the building on the pretext of looking for Louise.

He'd been in the main reception area once before, and the heavy gilt, red brocade, and mahogany decor was just as overpowering as before. Now he glanced into the two smaller chapels, which were done in ethereal tones of ice blue and white, with lace curtains shrouding the windows and floral display stands lined up along the walls like sentinels.

Farther down the hall he found an austere but tasteful office obviously meant for doing business with clients, with a discreet black leather folder placed neatly on the desk and a simple, two-drawer file cabinet in the corner. Through a second doorway inside, he caught a glimpse of the casket showroom.

Moving on down the hallway he discovered a stairwell, an elevator, a locked storeroom of some kind—interesting, that—and a coatroom.

So beyond the main-floor storeroom, anything of interest had to be on the second floor or downstairs. He scanned the area, called Louise's name quietly just to cover his bases, then eased the stairwell door open.

What had probably been a servants' passageway in the early days of this fine old home, the stairs were narrow and lit by fluorescent lights that hummed and flickered as he slipped up to the second floor.

Louise would likely be up here, he figured, and perhaps Gene, as well, but a workman coming up for further instructions wouldn't be out of the ordinary. Just figuring out the layout would be helpful enough.

At the next landing he peered up into the gloom, where the stairs narrowed even more, and only an incandescent bulb lit the way up to the attic. *Later*.

When he opened the door to the second floor, Gene's agitated voice filtered down the hall. A pause—then the voice grew higher with obvious stress. But damn—what was Gene saying?

A polished oak hallway bisected this floor, with four doors leading off to either side. Only the one at the far end was open—a different room than he'd briefly been in before. He stopped to listen for a second, then moved quietly down the hallway and stopped just out of sight.

"No—it will be okay. I promise," Gene exclaimed. "Just like usual. No surprises. I *swear*. I—"

"Joe! Are you up here? Joe!" Louise's voice warbled up the back staircase and set his teeth on edge.

Oh God, not now.

But then he heard a step creak, and from inside Gene's office came the sound of a phone receiver slamming down. A split second later he appeared at his office door, his face flushed and his eyes hard. "Why are you up here?" he demanded. "These are private offices."

"Sorry—I was just looking for Louise. Is there anything else you want me to do?"

The woman arrived at the top of the stairs at that moment. She gave him a wink and a smile. "I'm sure we can find lots of jobs for you around here."

"WHAT WE HAVE HERE," Fred said solemnly, "is the biggest failure to communicate since the Titanic went down."

Catherine spared him a brief glance, then turned her attention back to the crocheting in her lap. "You exaggerate, Frederick. You always have. Why, when you were a boy—"

Fred paced to the other side of the parlor, then turned on his heel and pulled to a stop in front of her. "I'm talking about now, Cathy, not the Dark Ages."

"Catherine."

"Well, you weren't always this stuffy. I remember our senior-class trip, and—"

"That," she sniffed, "was a long, *long* time ago."

He sighed heavily. "I have tried for a long time. But you like that high horse you're on better than coming to earth for something real."

"I have *no* idea what you're talking about."

He shook his head sadly. "No, I guess you don't. I'm giving up. I know you don't care either way, but I just have to say it."

She made another complicated crochet stitch without looking up. "Giving up what?"

He threw up his hands in frustration. "See? Them books about Mars and Venus are right. You *are* on another planet. And after this, I'm not trying to make that trip again. If you want me, you need to try. I'm done."

That got her attention. "Is that an *ultimatum?*" When he threw her a disgusted look and stomped out of the parlor, she snorted. "I hardly need an ultimatum from you or anyone else."

Abby watched Catherine attack her crocheting with hook and fingers flying, then shook her head and went back into the kitchen to check the seasoning in the spaghetti sauce she'd had in the slow cooker all day.

After long hours at her college classes, coming home to a hot meal was like being a kid again, back when Mom had supper ready every night. Listening to Fred and Catherine bicker was like the old days, too, when she used to hear the constant arguing among her younger sisters, but the nostalgia wasn't quite as sweet.

Joe strolled into the kitchen, dressed in khakis and a snug black polo shirt, with a gold watch gleaming at his tanned wrist and hair damp from a shower. For just a second, she almost forgot to breathe.

"You're usually not around this early," he said. "Playing hooky?"

"My two-hour social-welfare policies class was canceled, and I always have a free hour before it. I figured I could work on supper and then get a good start on revising my research proposal." She reached for the crushed basil and oregano containers on the counter and added a pinch of each to the sauce. "You're not usually so dressed up. What gives?"

"Megan's teacher."

Abby's stomach did a little flip-flop. "Ahhhh."

"An *appointment*," he added.

An unexpected sense of relief washed through her. Which was ridiculous, because she had no hold on him. Maybe she thought about him—a lot—and imagined a little too much, but the man was free and clear to flirt with anyone.

"So what do you think about how Megan's adjusting here?"

"I thought she was doing well enough. But she

wrote a really sad poem in school about losing her mother, and...I don't know.'' He opened his hands, palms up. ''The teacher wants to talk about it.''

''What did Megan say in the poem?''

''That only her mother loved her, and nobody else even cares about her.'' Joe shook his head. ''I figure she'll miss her mother all her life, and I know it had to be hard leaving Carl's place. But I figured she was doing okay with me.''

''Surely now she sees how much you love her?''

''God, I hope so. I'm still new at this hands-on parenting stuff, but I'm sure trying.''

Abby tasted the sauce again, savoring the spicy Italian blend. She picked up the salt. ''Is she coming with you?''

''She's still at school. The principal's secretary will have her wait in the office, in case we need to talk to her.''

He looked so concerned that she easily slipped into her social-worker-to-be mode and took his hand. She realized her mistake when his eyes widened, but she doggedly plowed ahead, trying to ignore the warmth of his hand in hers. And then she felt his long, strong fingers curl around hers.

''It's...um...not easy being a parent under any conditions. Maybe you weren't around when she was younger, but I think you're doing a great job.''

He stood even closer now, and his gaze drifted down to her lips. ''Thanks.''

''With those two boys, too. I never would have guessed that any kid with orange-dyed hair and that many body rings would work so hard.'' Self-conscious now, she tried to step back, but he kept a gentle grip on her hand, and drew her closer instead.

''They're good kids who just need a little direction.'' A smile played at the corners of his mouth. ''But thanks for the vote of confidence.''

Her own confidence was slipping fast. There'd been a humid breeze this morning, followed by light rain, and her hair had gone wild. Any makeup she'd applied this morning had to be long gone. So why was he looking down at her in that heavy-lidded way?

''Maybe this isn't appropriate,'' he murmured. ''But I sure as hell have wanted to do this for a long, long time.''

The first kiss feathered across her lips, sending tingles racing through her nerve fibers. The second one lasted longer—and suddenly the room spun out of sight and she found herself opening to him, absorbing the heat of him as she leaned into him asking for even more.

Disoriented, with sparks of awareness and heat

still licking through her veins, she abruptly found herself standing two feet away from him, with his hands braced on her shoulders. His force reflected the shock and awareness and desire she felt.

"Oh," she whispered.

He stared back at her, his forehead creased, as if he, too, was stunned.

"Maybe that wasn't such a good idea."

"Maybe not."

"There's really no future in this, you know."

"I'm well aware."

"It would be too awkward, living in the same house, with all the others here."

"Absolutely."

His gaze flicked up to the clock on the wall. "I'm sorry. Guess I'd better go."

"Of course," she said firmly. "And don't worry. As far as I'm concerned, this never happened."

She waited until she heard him go out the front door, then she sagged against the stove. Deciding his kiss had never happened would be like denying that the sun rose every day.

Never had she been kissed like that. Never had she felt such an overwhelming need to take a simple kiss and see how far it could go.

But now she knew. Distance would need to be

the only thing between them, from now on, because taking things any further would be like playing with fire.

MISS DARBY WAS WAITING for Joe at the front desk when he walked in. So was the principal, Mrs. Miller, a portly, gray-haired woman with the stern expression of an old-school nun. Neither pair of eyes left his face from the minute he walked in the door.

The principal gestured toward a door behind the school secretary's desk.

"We can talk in my office, Mr. Coughlin," she said. "The bell will ring in five minutes, and there's more privacy in here."

He'd planned and staged drug raids. Gone undercover to investigate suspects who'd just as soon shoot someone in the gut as wait for an explanation. This morning he'd blandly faced down both Gene and Louise, with an offhand explanation that he was upstairs at the funeral home, because he was trying to find Louise.

But walking into the world of elementary education with these two women on his heels made him feel as if he was eight years old and in trouble.

He settled onto one of the hard wooden chairs placed in front of the principal's desk and noted with amusement that the principal's chair sat much higher—a good intimidation tactic, no doubt, for the problem kids who needed extra intervention.

"Nice office," he said, glancing at the wall filled with framed certificates and group photographs of children identified by year with engraved silver plaques.

"Thank you, Mr. Coughlin." Mrs. Miller tapped a stack of files on her desktop into perfect alignment. "To get right to the point, Miss Darby is concerned about your daughter, and has talked to me on several occasions. Megan has just been here a little over two weeks, but we wanted to visit with you before things go any further."

"Go any further?" he growled. "That sounds ominous."

"What we mean," Miss Darby said quickly, "is that we're *worried* about Megan. She's so…well, withdrawn. She won't join into discussions, and isn't very cooperative. When we have a test, she may not even try to finish it. And her papers…"

"It's tough changing schools," he said. "At the end of the year like this, it's even harder. Maybe I should have just kept her at home."

Mrs. Miller rolled a pencil between her fingers and looked at him over the top of her reading glasses. "Of course, change is hard, but I don't think it's the key issue here. I was a school counselor for years before becoming a principal. She's written some rather disturbing assignments in the

two weeks we've had her. Coupled with her attitude…''

''Considering all she has been through, her attitude is amazing.'' Feeling as if he was defending
his little girl against the world, Joe braced his elbows on the arms of his chair and steepled his
fingers. ''I talked about all of this with Miss Darby,
here, when Megan first came to class.'' He glanced
in her direction. ''Remember?''

''We don't mean to seem confrontational, Mr.
Coughlin,'' the principal said gently. She thumbed
open the top folder on her desk and lifted out one
of the pages. ''You told us that Megan lived with
her mother and stepfather after your divorce.''

''That's right. My job involved a lot of travel. I
thought it was best for her, at the time.''

''And then there was the accident, and Megan
lived with her aunt and uncle for several years until
her aunt became ill.''

Joe nodded.

''And then there's your…'' Mrs. Miller paused
delicately. ''Background.''

Joe's mouth fell open. Straightening up in his
chair, he gave her a hard look. ''My *what?*''

''Rumors, of course, but they all seem to origi-
nate with your daughter.''

Joe stifled a curse. He'd been so careful, wanting
to protect Megan from the knowledge of his in-

carceration. Even before that, she'd never really known about his career, because he hadn't wanted her to be scared about the risks he took. And no one—not one person except his brother in California—knew why he was in town.

"I'm not sure what you mean," he said evenly.

The two women exchanged glances.

"Megan has written some rather tall tales. She seems to think you're quite an action hero—wielding a gun, fighting for justice—there was one story about a motorcycle gang terrorizing a small town…"

He nearly laughed aloud with relief. "That's *it?*"

"It's hardly amusing," Mrs. Miller said firmly, "if your daughter is making up an entire fantasy world and sharing it with others as the truth. She read several papers in front of the class, and the other children were enthralled."

Joe briefly relayed the incident with the bikers at the gas station, playing down his role and elevating the youthful attendant to star status.

"I only helped, but I'm sure it was a terrifying experience for Megan. Here she was, away from the family she'd come to love, heading for a new home with a dad she barely remembered. Maybe it made her feel more secure to think that I'm invincible."

"At least that explains things," the principal conceded. "We'd been worried that…well…"

"But we know it's not true, of course." A faint rosy blush crept into Miss Darby's cheeks.

So they'd had his record checked out, and his identity had held firm. *Thank you, Carl.* "I guess Megan and I have some serious talking to do."

Megan's stories probably explained why the other parents had given him such wary glances at the school open house. Given how children could embellish a good tale, they'd all probably thought they were facing a modern-day Jesse James.

"There's still the issue of Megan's well-being. I believe the poetry she wrote shows signs of depression."

He suddenly felt way out of his depth. "Depression?"

"We can probably get her scheduled with the district school psychologist for an evaluation by the end of May. Even over the summer, there would be services available for her in Winthrop, where the main offices are."

"We'll be back in California by mid-June, and will be staying close to her uncle and aunt. If things are going well—" He winced. "Well, maybe she'll want to be with them again, with her cousins and all. I only want what's best for her."

Mrs. Miller held his gaze for a long moment,

then she stood and extended her hand. "Since Megan only has a short time left here, we'll keep a close eye on her and do all we can. If anything changes, we'll contact you immediately and pursue that outside evaluation."

When Joe walked out of the office, Megan was waiting for him on a chair by the secretary's desk, her shoulders slumped.

When she saw him, her eyes filled with tears. "A-am I in big trouble?"

He wanted to scoop her up into his arms and give her a bear hug, and soothe away her fears. But other children filled the crowded hall just beyond the office door and he didn't want to embarrass her. Instead, he sat next to her and draped an arm over her shoulders. "You aren't in trouble."

"B-but Miss Darby said…" Her voice trailed off.

"We just need to talk about a few things when we get home—nothing serious. Then we can start talking about going back to California a few weeks after school is over for the summer." He pulled away enough so he could look down at her. The next words were the hardest ones he'd ever had to say. "Is that what you want, to be back with Carl and Bonnie?"

She silently studied the toes of her Nikes. Finally, a lifetime later, she looked up at him and

searched his face. His heart faltered when she
started to speak.

"Yeah. That would be the best."

He'd wanted her to say no. To say that she loved
him and wanted to stay with him instead, but what
could he expect? She couldn't remember all the
good times up until she was four—and after that,
she'd been in her mother's custody or with Carl.
Of course she would choose Carl, and she was
right to do so.

With Joe, she'd have no siblings to play with,
no mom to tuck her in at night. He'd never again
take away from her the only security she knew.

CHAPTER NINE

MEGAN DAWDLED on the way home from school. Down the block, she could see Dad lingering at the hedge along the sidewalk, trimming stray twigs, but really just watching for her to come. *As if he cares.* He'd sure made that clear enough yesterday after school.

She'd sat on that chair staring at the closed door to the principal's office, and it had felt as if she had six hamsters chasing each other in her stomach. Things had to be bad—really bad—if the principal had called him in. "I didn't even *do* anything!" she muttered, scuffing her toes against the cracks in the sidewalk.

Nothing except sit like a lump at her desk, feeling shy and embarrassed and totally out of place. After school she had Lindsey and sometimes Aimee. In class—nobody. And now Dad was ready to get rid of her as soon as they left this place.

The funny thing was that she'd once wanted exactly that—to go back to her cousins, the big old house in Sacramento, and her friends down the street. Dad didn't hug her all the time like Aunt Bonnie had, or tease her like Uncle Carl. He didn't know about Old Maid and Crazy Eights and how to braid her hair.

Yet…she'd started feeling as though it was right, being with him. And now he didn't want her at all.

"Megan! Wait up!"

At the sound of footsteps racing up behind her, she turned to find Aimee coming at a run, her blond pigtails bouncing as she pulled to a gangly stop. Megan's heart lifted. "Can you come over?"

"No. I…" Aimee fell in step with her, biting her lower lip. "I tried to find you before school, but I got there late and the bell rang." Her eyes filled with sudden tears. "I…um…need a favor."

Megan had been feeling miserable, but Aimee looked even worse. "What happened?"

"It's Buffy. My dad was home last night reading the newspaper, and he looked up and saw Buffy with his best pair of shoes. Do you know how *fast* a puppy can destroy shoes?"

Megan had a pretty good idea—Buffy loved to wrestle, and his teeth were like needles. "What did he say?"

"First he grabbed the shoe and took it to his bedroom…then he yelled so loud we all thought there was a fire." Aimee looked away. "He stepped right in a pile of puppy poo with his bare feet. And, he found his other shoe with its toe chewed, too. He told my mom that Buffy was… um…the 'spawn of Satan' and had to go.''

''But he'll get over it, right? Like you said before?''

A tear trickled down Aimee's cheek. ''Not this time.''

''He's gonna sell Buffy?''

''Worse. He said he wasn't going to wait for any newspaper ad, hoping someone might come to buy Buffy, while our house was being destroyed. After work tonight he's taking him to the pound.''

Megan stared at her, horrified. ''Where they might *kill* him?''

Aimee nodded, her tears flowing freely now. ''Remember when that animal-rescue lady came to school? She said they tried hard, but could never find enough homes. Please—can you take him? I don't want him to die!''

They'd reached the front of Abby's house. Dad smiled at them both from the other side of the hedge. ''Did you have a good day at school, girls?''

''*Ask* him,'' Aimee whispered, giving Megan an elbow in the side.

''Please!''

Right. Like he was going to do her a favor. He'd

talked to her last night about telling the truth, and not making up stories about him being what he wasn't, and her cheeks still burned when she thought about what he'd said. It was probably a big reason why he didn't want her—who wanted a kid like that?

Megan glanced uncertainly between Aimee and Dad. "If you could save someone from dying, would you do it?"

A sad shadow came into his eyes, as if he was remembering something from a long time ago. "I think anyone would try, honey. Why do you ask?"

"So if it was life and death, even for someone— or something—really small, you'd try."

"Are we talking people here?"

She took a deep breath. "Puppies."

"Ah." He reached out with the clippers in his hand and snapped off another twig.

"A beautiful, fun, happy puppy," she rushed on. "Like Buffy."

He gave her the kind of patient smile Carl always used when he was trying to be nice about saying no. "For that you need a place of your own. A fenced yard. It's a lot of responsibility, Megan— food, water, vet bills, shots, a kennel and lots of time, too."

"M-my dad says Buffy has to go to the animal shelter," Aimee said brokenly.

"He'll be put to sleep."

"Oh, not a nice puppy like Buffy. Someone will come along and—"

"No! The lady talked at our school. She said that doesn't always happen. Please—can I give him to Megan?" Aimee pleaded. "She likes him a lot, and he likes her, too."

"Please, Dad? Please? He could even stay out in the garage, but I bet Hamlet would like a playmate. I would take care of him before and after school."

His eyes twinkling, Dad held his hands up as if warding off an attack. "I believe you. I remember how much I wanted a puppy when I was a kid. But we'll be moving a long ways off in a month or so." When Aimee and Megan both started to speak at once, he shook his head. "I'm sorry, but it isn't even up to me. Abby owns this house, and I doubt she'd want all of her boarders coming home with new pets. If we got one, how fair would that be to the others who live here?"

"I can't see Fred or Catherine ever wanting a pet," Megan grumbled. "They don't even like *themselves*."

"But what about Sue and Lindsey? And then think about your aunt Bonnie. Will she be up to having a puppy underfoot?"

His words made her feel like the time she'd gone

too high on the swings and jumped off, knocking the breath out of her lungs. She'd sprawled on the ground, gasping for air like a beached fish. He didn't seem to mind at all the thought of dumping her off, and that hurt.

"Since you don't want me, it would be nice to have *something* that could be just mine," she cried, rushing past him to the front porch.

"Wait!"

She heard him, but she didn't care.

JOE WATCHED HER race up the steps and disappear into the house, then turned back to Aimee who still stood by the hedge, looking acutely embarrassed.

"I guess that didn't go so well," he said dryly, bracing his hands on his hips. "I'm really sorry about the puppy. If this was our house...well... things might be different."

"Yeah." Her shoulders slumped.

"Surely some nice family will take him home."

"M-maybe Buffy will be one of the lucky ones."

Her accusing, tear-filled eyes were truly pathetic as she started up the street.

I sure handled that well.

In prison, he'd thought about his daughter day and night. He'd imagined what she looked like, because the photos Carl sent were never enough.

He'd wondered what she liked to do. What it would be like talking to her, getting to know her. He'd figured that he would get settled in a decent place, find a job, and bring her home, and that being a parent would be an *adventure*.

He hadn't expected that he'd be such a failure at it.

Peeling off his gloves, he watched Aimee until she turned up Lark Street and disappeared behind the Foleys' shrubbery.

Abby met him on the front porch. "How's everything going?"

Another failure—Abby Hilliard. He'd kissed her yesterday, against all of his principles, and since then she'd occupied most of his thoughts, leading to an unexpected revelation: her late husband must have been crazy to have lost interest in his all-too-enticing young wife.

Just the memory of that kiss warmed him in places that had been cold for a long, long time. Even clad in gray sweatpants and a sweatshirt, she was one of the sexiest women he'd ever seen.

"Things are…fair."

She gave him a knowing look. "And Megan?"

He tossed the hedge clippers into the box of tools he'd left on the steps and jammed his hands into his back pockets.

"It's probably safe to say that she and her friend think I'm the biggest ogre in Silver Springs."

"Both of them? Now *that's* bad. What happened? She just ran up to her room like the world was going to end."

"Aimee's puppy. Apparently her dad is taking it to the humane shelter tonight."

"Let me guess—the girls figure Megan could take the puppy and save him." She eyed Joe thoughtfully. "But you didn't think it was a good idea."

"Exactly."

She moved to the end of the porch and sat in one of the white wicker chairs by the porch swing. "A puppy is a lot of work."

He followed and dropped into the porch swing in front of her, their knees nearly touching. He was thankful just to have someone to talk to. "Yes, it is. And with Megan in school and me doing odd jobs for you and Gene, the dog would be neglected. It's also one extra responsibility that I just can't take on right now."

Leaning back in her chair, she stared up at the pale blue porch ceiling.

"Buffy is an awfully nice pup."

He nearly groaned. "Not you, too."

"I'm just saying—he's quite a sweetie. Goldens are energetic as puppies, but he'll probably be a gentle old soul in a couple of years.'' She rolled her head against the back cushion to look at Joe. ''Where will you be in a year or so? In your own home?''

''Probably. But I don't know where.''

''Maybe a dog would be good for Megan. She's had a lot of changes in her life. He could be a good companion for her—something consistent, while she's getting used to your new place, and new friends.''

There was compassion and concern in her voice, nothing judgmental, but he felt a flash of guilt all the same. Which was ridiculous. Megan had made her wishes clear. He'd even asked her a second time, while listening to her prayers last night, and she'd said the same thing.

''When we leave here, she's going back to live with her aunt and uncle.''

''You're kidding.'' Abby leveled her gaze on him. ''You're her *father*.''

''To her, that's in name only.'' He gave a bitter laugh. ''And I guess that doesn't apply, either, does it? She's been Megan Graham since she was five.''

''On her first night here, Megan mentioned it. I think it still bothers her a lot.''

He measured his words, carefully holding back all the old anger and frustration that simmered through him at the memory. "Back then I was…in a bad place, emotionally. When her stepdad wanted to adopt her, it seemed like the best thing for Megan. She'd have a dad, they'd all have the same name, and she could feel like she belonged. At the time I didn't think I'd ever be able to be a part of her life again."

Actually, at the time, he'd been serving twenty years without parole on trumped-up federal drug charges, knowing he would miss Megan's entire childhood, though Abby probably thought he was alluding to a struggle with mental illness.

Maybe he was. Because the day he'd agreed to let his daughter go had been the day he nearly gave up on life itself. No slam of a judge's gavel, no clang of a prison door, could have done more to rob him of all hope. His grief had evolved into anger, then rage—and the first con who'd tried to strong-arm him into submission earned a fast trip to the hospital with a broken jaw and two broken ribs.

Maybe that's what had kept him alive, because after that, most of the others had given him respect and a wide berth, though he'd never quit watching his back.

And though he'd been careful to leash his anger after that day, it still seethed through his veins.

Five years. *Five* horrific years of his life…and the guys responsible were still free.

"Are you sure she wants to go back with her aunt and uncle?" Abby's voice jarred Joe back into the present.

"That's what she says." *And God knows I don't want to hurt her any more than I already have.*

Abby moved to the edge of her seat and leaned forward to wrap his hands in hers. "You're a good man, Joe. Caring, and honest, and she's a very lucky girl to have you for her dad."

Her touch was light, but he felt it all the way to his bones, and he prayed she wouldn't see the guilt in his eyes. The whole reason for his presence here was a lie. Everything she knew about him was untrue, and he couldn't do one thing right now to change that fact.

Yet…he found himself curving a hand behind her head and drawing her closer, until his mouth brushed lightly against hers.

The impact sent a raw sweep of desire through him so powerful that without thought, he deepened that kiss until everything else just fell away. All logic. All caution.

It wasn't until he felt the gentle pressure of her hands against his chest that he finally regained his focus.

She stared at him, her cheeks pink and her wide hazel eyes dark and soft and stunned. "Holy Hannah, do you *always* kiss like that?"

Only with you, Abby. It took a second to gather his scattered thoughts and remember how to stand, but then he gave the most casual shrug he could muster. "Guess I'd better go upstairs and talk to Megan, and mend a few fences."

He was halfway through the front door when he heard her wicker chair creak against the wooden floor of the porch. "Hamlet could use a little buddy for a while," she called out. "Just in case you're wondering."

It wasn't just the puppy that he was wondering about, Joe thought with a grim smile after he found the number he needed and made a quick call from Abby's kitchen.

There'd been a busy visitation this morning at the Sheltering Pines, and an overflow crowd for the funeral in the late afternoon, so he hadn't been able to do any more work on the windows as a cover for entering the building.

He needed to get back inside to check Gene's caller ID before there were too many more calls on it. He needed to keep his focus.

And he definitely needed to keep his distance from Abby Hilliard.

AFTER TRYING to talk to Megan yesterday—a one-sided effort, because she'd mostly just stared at her hands—he'd slipped away after supper and driven to the Wal-Mart in Winthrop for some supplies, then he'd stowed his purchases away and helped her with homework until it was time for her bath and bed.

This morning, though, dawned bright and sunny, a perfect day for exterior painting…and other things.

Over the past two weeks he'd had a good opportunity to observe Gene's and Louise's routines. Louise seemed to enjoy having Joe around and frequently came up with jobs for him.

Today, from eight-thirty until ten, Louise would go to her weekly hair appointment. Gene, who attended the Wednesday Morning Men's Prayer Breakfast at Saint Theresa's, wouldn't roll in until nine-fifteen.

Which meant that once Megan left for school with Sue and Lindsey, Joe had exactly forty-five minutes of freedom in the Sheltering Pines. The dismal office he'd been in before was promising, with that cluttered desk and the boxes stacked in the corner. But the one he needed to search most was Gene's office.

He was halfway across the backyard when he heard Fred call his name. Stifling a growl of impatience, he turned and looked back at the house.

"What do you need?"

Fred, his face unshaven and his wispy gray hair uncombed, stepped off the back porch and strolled across the lawn, a cup of coffee steaming in his hand. "Gotta busy day?" he drawled, shading his eyes to look up at the sun.

"Looks like a good one."

"I need to take advantage of it. I'm supposed to start painting the second-floor trim next door."

Fred chuckled and gestured onward with his cup. "Don't let me hold you back. I'll just come along and watch a bit."

Joe clenched and relaxed his hands at his sides. "I thought you usually ran deliveries during the day. And what about your taxi service?"

"Things are a mite slow. Anyway, I sorta lost my fire lately." He squinted at Joe through his thick bifocals. "There don't seem to be much point, you know?"

Joe stopped and turned to face him. "You're not feeling good?"

"Did you ever feel useless—like you were going nowhere? Like you wasted a lot of time you could never get back?" Fred chugged a long swallow of coffee. "It's hell."

"I thought you were doing okay."

"Worked twenty years as a ranch hand out at the Triple T; then another twenty for the feed mill." He gave a gusty sigh and threw the rest of his coffee out onto the lawn. "A little pension, a decent trailer with a nice view of a good trout stream…figured I was set till the day I died."

The old guy was in the mood to talk, and Joe knew Fred would probably follow him right on over to the funeral home and stand at the base of the ladder to continue if he didn't have his chance now. "What happened?"

"The days get long when you're alone. Me and the bottle had quite an affair going—had a little fire out there one day and that trailer was gone." He shook his head ruefully. "Lucky to be alive, but then my daughter got all riled—said I needed to be looked after 'cause I didn't eat right and drank too much. She badgered me until I moved to town. Said I could live like a hermit, but then I'd never see my grandson again."

"It isn't so bad here, is it?"

Fred snorted. "Okay—except for the company I've gotta keep."

"Ah." Joe had seen Catherine's haughty glares across the dinner table, and had heard Fred grumbling to himself during the last few days. In place of their usual bickering, there was now cold silence. "You two go way back, I take it."

"First grade. 'Course, I only made it through sixth, then I had to go to work at the Triple T to help out my ma. Cathy was townfolk—the banker's daughter. She got way too big for her britches after she went to college.''

''That happens.'' Fred seemed ready to share his whole life history, so Joe glanced pointedly at his watch. ''Sorry—I've got to leave you now, or I won't get my work done. Gene is a particular guy.''

''*Peculiar*, you mean,'' Fred chortled. ''Last thing I'd ever want to do is sleep in a funeral home!''

Joe stilled. ''He *stays* there?'' The circular driveway wrapped around the building and the garages were at the far end of the property, so cars could come and go without being noticed from Abby's house. He'd seen Gene coming and going at all hours, but never with any regularity except for his Wednesday-morning meeting.

''There's a small apartment upstairs, but he's also got a house on the other side of town. One of them fancy new houses.'' Fred lifted his empty cup in salute. ''You know, sometimes I get the feeling there's a lot more to you than you let on.''

''Really?''

After a slow perusal with narrowed eyes, Fred gave him a sly wink. ''You're too sharp to be wastin' your life, not doing anything. I don't know who you are, but you're not a no-account drifter.

Maybe you'll stick around for good. Get a good job, and be the one who takes good care of our Abby.''

''She's a good woman.''

''See that you remember that, son. A good one like her is hard to find.'' Appearing pleased with himself, Fred nodded. ''*Real* hard. See you at dinnertime.''

Joe lifted a hand in farewell, vaulted over the low brick wall and headed for the storage building where the ladder and painting supplies were kept. In minutes he was up on the ladder at the same window of the office he'd been in once before, with the removable screen window taken down and a bucket of white paint in his hand.

Testing the lower window sash, he smiled to himself. He'd guessed right—now he knew Gene's office was at the end of the hall, and this room probably wasn't used often. No one had thought to lock the window since he'd been up here last.

Surveying the backyard below and the properties to either side for any onlookers, he lifted the lower window sash higher and slipped inside.

The weedy-looking plant was still there, the desk was still cluttered, and the jumbled stack of boxes appeared to be untouched since the last time.

Donning a pair of gloves, Joe silently crossed the room and tried the door handle. It was locked, as before, but today he had time, and now he had the tools.

Grabbing a thin case from his hip pocket, he first studied the lock, then selected a slender torque wrench and a snake-tip pick from his set. In less than five seconds he was out of the room.

The old mansion was dark and still, with the soft, musty odor he'd detected once before, like that of an old library. He listened for any activity, then toed off his running shoes and moved down the hardwood-floored hallway to the end, where he found Gene's door locked—but just as easy to breach.

Out of habit, he scanned the room for surveillance equipment before stepping inside. Unlikely, yet he'd seen some pretty sophisticated security and defense measures used in drug operations— often more advanced than what the good guys used—and if Gene was heavily involved, it would pay to be cautious.

Eight-forty.

Moving more quickly now, Joe crossed over to the desk, grabbed a notebook from his pocket and started scrolling through the phone numbers on the caller ID. It still amazed—and gratified—him when a suspect left his entire phone history for God and anyone to see, and Gene was no sharper than some of the other suspects who'd inadvertently assisted his investigations in the past.

He reviewed the incoming call data, writing down the names and numbers, and jotting hash marks beside those who had called more than once, until he got to Monday morning. Two unknown callers—no name, no number. Damn. He continued checking back through a dozen calls, a sinking feeling in his stomach...

Then he froze, and excitement flickered through him at the number on the screen. No name, but it was a long distance number with a Colorado area code, and the timing was about right. Could this be the source of the agitated conversation he'd overheard?

He scanned the rest of the numbers, writing fast, then jammed the notebook in his back pocket and powered on Gene's desktop computer. He bypassed the password with several deft keystrokes.

Excel...the database...he glanced at the clock and cursed under his breath. *Nine o'clock.*

Edgy now, he shoved a disk into the A drive and began copying database files, his frustration rising at the slow processor. Any minute now, and Louise would be back...Gene could return early...

From downstairs came the sound of a door creaking open. Footsteps coming down the hall toward the stairs.

The doorway at the bottom of the stairs opened.

Without bothering to close out of the program, he grabbed his disk and pushed the off button on the computer. He gave the room a quick survey, then silently rushed down the hall and slipped into the room he'd entered. Locked the door behind him.

A second later, the hinges of the second-floor stairwell squealed open.

Home free, he muttered as he grabbed the paint and paintbrush and escaped through the window.

He had more to go on now—phone numbers he could search on the Internet. A lot of names. But it was just a start, and he needed to get back in there to get a good look at the rest of that computer—and what was in those file drawers, too.

Because he'd bet his boots that Gene Hilliard had a lot to hide.

CHAPTER TEN

SHE'D FIRST THOUGHT he was just a handsome drifter—one of those sad souls unable to settle down into a steady job or a strong family relationship. Yesterday, he'd alluded to having problems that had made him give up his daughter, and her first thought had been drugs, booze or mental illness.

But watching him now—as he drove the last staple into the woven wire fencing at the far end of her property—she couldn't imagine him with any of those problems. He was lean, tanned and muscular, with the purposeful stride of someone who made plans and carried them out. He worked hard, and he had a way of looking her straight in the eye that sent shivers down her spine and made her believe he had nothing at all to hide.

He was the biggest enigma she'd come across in a long while. "So," she ventured, "what's it been like, being out on the road?"

He picked up the sack of staples and shoved the hammer into the tool belt slung low at his hip. "I always wanted to travel. What have you always wanted to do?''

She *wanted* to sit him down and do a social history on him and find out what made him tick. To find out where he'd been, and why, and if he was going to simply drift forever or if this was just a phase. But her fledgling interview skills hadn't gotten her to first base. ''Have you seen any areas where you'd like to settle down?'' she persisted.

''A few.'' His smile didn't reach his eyes. ''But I'll end up close to Sacramento so I can see Megan as often as I can.''

He was still alluding to sending his daughter back to her aunt and uncle, clearly sacrificing his own wishes in an effort to give her what she wanted. And it was such a mistake—one Abby hoped to resolve before he left town.

But now she tactfully changed the subject. ''She's going to be one happy girl when she gets home from school today.''

''You're sure it's okay to have the puppy here?'' He surveyed the backyard. ''Buffy has a checkered past.''

''He'll have a safe, fenced backyard to romp in now, and she can keep him in a portable kennel in her room at night if she wants. I think he'll do her a lot of good.''

''I hope so. God knows she hasn't had it easy.'' He glanced impatiently at his watch as they walked to the garage. "We've still got another thirty minutes before school's out."

She found his boyish anticipation impossibly sweet. "Want some lemonade while you wait?"

Sometimes, when she offered just a simple thing—like lemonade or warm cookies, or an evening walk to the Dairy Queen for the three of them, there would be a faraway expression on his face, as if he was remembering sad times, but she'd never seen a more appreciative man.

The combination made her want to wrap her arms around him and hold him close…though she'd already learned what happened when she got too close to Joe Coughlin. He made her pulse race and her blood heat, and made her forget everything, including her common sense.

Now, though, he surprised her by turning down her offer. "Maybe I should run over to the Colwells'."

"You could," she agreed, trying not to smile. "But they're just a few blocks away. It won't take long."

"True." He put the supplies away in the garage and shut the door, and they both walked over to the back porch and sat on the top step. "You didn't tell me yet—what have you always wanted to do?"

"Right now? I have three term papers due next week, and finals the week after that. I want to finish school at the end of summer term."

"And then?"

"I'll be moving, I hope."

He shifted sideways and looked down at her. "Moving?"

"Far."

"What about this great old house? Your boarders?"

"The house isn't fully mine. And the boarders? You already plan to leave, and the rest of them know. Sue needs a ground-floor apartment, anyway. Catherine is talking about another room-and-board facility in town that's closer to the Senior Center. And Fred—I don't know. He swears he wants to move back out to the foothills into another trailer, but his daughter says no."

Joe cocked his head. "I just figured this was the house you and your husband owned."

"In a manner of speaking." She gave a vague wave of her hand. "You know what? It's about time to watch for Megan. I'll do that so you can go, okay?"

She watched him jog down the street, a new leash coiled in his hand, then she waited out in front of the house.

If there were prizes for dawdling, Megan surely would have earned first place. Five minutes later she appeared in front of the school at the far end of the street. She picked up dandelions. Clacked a stick against a picket fence as she walked past a house at the end of the block. Stopped to take off her shoes.

When she finally arrived, Abby hid a smile. "Young lady, I need to show you something."

Surprise and wariness sharpened Megan's sullen expression. "I didn't do anything wrong, did I?"

"No…but you need to come with me to the backyard."

"Why?"

"Your dad wants to see you."

"Oh."

"Honey, I know moving here was hard on you. But he's trying hard to be a good dad."

"Yeah."

Her lack of enthusiasm made Abby want to take her shoulders and give her a little shake. "You need to give him a chance. This isn't easy for him, either, you know."

"Then he should have left me with Uncle Carl."

When they rounded the corner of the house and walked through the gate, the backyard was empty. And then, from behind the garage came a flash of golden fur heading straight for Megan. Joe appeared, too, but he held back, leaned a hip against the building and watched.

Megan knelt to the grass and caught Buffy with open arms as he wiggled and whined and licked her face. "Why are you here, buddy? Did you get lost?'' She laughed, fending off the pup's eager kisses.

"He's yours, Megan," Joe said quietly.

Her mouth fell open. "Mine?" Her voice rose to a squeal. "He's mine?"

"As long as you take good care of him."

The puppy squirmed in her arms, his wagging tail a blur, then he pulled away and ran through the yard in dizzying circles until he found a twig to pick up. He raced back to her with his prize.

She gathered him up in her arms and stood, then went to where her father stood, her head bowed. "I...um...wasn't very nice the other day."

"That's okay, honey. I understand."

He didn't make a move toward her, though, and Abby's heart turned over at the sight of father and daughter, standing awkwardly apart, both wary and hurting.

After a long moment, Megan lifted her head. "I know you didn't want to get him. If...you did it because of the mean things I said..." She swallowed hard. "You didn't have to."

"I want you to be happy. And I thought you could use a friend."

After that, it took only a heartbeat. Megan put the puppy down, laughing when he found another twig and raced off. Then she looked up at her father with shining eyes and walked into his embrace.

THE HOUSE WASN'T QUIET until after eleven that night.

Megan, overexcited by the puppy, hadn't fallen asleep until ten, and then Buffy must have whined in his kennel, awakening her. When Joe checked in on them ten minutes later, he found the pup snuggled contentedly at her side and her hugging him close.

A deep feeling of love and tenderness came over him at the sight of his little girl and her dog… along with an aching sense of loss. He'd lost so much time with her, and now he wanted to start over, in a real home, where he could give her the stable life she deserved. But his progress here in Silver Springs was far too slow.

Stifling a growl of impatience, he double-checked the lock on the bedroom door and set up his laptop and portable printer, then connected to the Internet.

Last night, the phone line had been busy until he finally gave up around one o'clock—Abby doing online research for one of her papers, maybe. And with just one phone line into the house, he hadn't wanted to risk using it during the day, when others might need the phone.

Now—finally—he accessed an Internet phone directory and began checking each of the phone numbers he'd copied from Gene's caller ID, writing down names and addresses.

In the past, as an agent he'd been able to contact the phone company for needed records, but now he was on his own. Until he found out who had set him up, he didn't dare ask any of his old buddies for help. Dealing with limited investigative resources was a whole lot better than being dead.

The phone numbers without caller name identification were easy enough, using a "reverse phone book" program to look up the corresponding names and addresses, but two of the numbers intrigued him. No name or address came up, but they were in the same Colorado code, with the last four digits identical.

And—given the time frame—one was probably the number of the caller who'd gotten Gene so upset.

Joe logged off the Internet, then loaded the disk he'd used in Gene's office. There hadn't been time to download all he'd been after, but satisfaction curled through him as he began reviewing what he'd managed to copy—Gene's contact database, neatly listed by category.

Vault companies.

Casket suppliers.

Floral suppliers.

Printing companies.

Embalming suppliers.

Paper-goods suppliers.

Leaning back in his chair, he idly tapped his pen

against the desk as he scrolled through the company names…then suddenly jerked to a halt, sat up straight, and scrolled back again.

Four of the six floral suppliers had the same out-of-state zip codes and the same first three digits as Monday morning's mystery caller. *Five* out of seven paper-goods suppliers were in the same area, as well.

And all but two were listed with post-office-box addresses.

He grinned as he studied the list of phone numbers he'd written down, then checked the area codes on the map in the front of the phone book on the desk. *Denver.*

There were a few Wyoming companies listed for each category, and maybe it was logical that a nearby metropolitan area would be the area of choice for doing business. But the proximity of those post-office-box addresses to one another was a red flag. And there'd been five calls from one of those numbers in the last few days.

He glanced at the clock. *Midnight.* A legitimate company would have an answering machine, or the phone would simply ring and ring.

Pulling a calling card from his billfold, he dialed the 800-number and his lengthy PIN on the back of the card, then dialed the number. With a paid calling card, it wouldn't be easy to trace his call.

The phone rang six, seven, eight times.

And then a drowsy voice growled a profanity equal to anything he had heard in prison.

"Yo," he returned in a low voice. "I'm just checkin' in, man."

"What?" The guy at the other end of the line sucked in a deep breath, his voice suddenly wary. "Who the hell is this?"

No one you need to know about just yet, Joe thought as he ended the call. *But soon you're going to be sorry that you answered that phone.*

"I'M SO SORRY," Gene murmured, shaking his head. "I can't believe I didn't notice the damage on that casket when it came in. I called the company to demand an adjustment in price."

"I wouldn't have noticed that scratch if you hadn't pointed it out," Mrs. Mendoz said, gripping a tissue in one hand. Her other hand wavered over her checkbook. "You can't imagine how much I appreciate your honesty. One hears such awful things about..." She colored slightly. "You know—funeral homes that take advantage."

"This is a family business. Our reputation means everything to us. And to steal from a grieving family, well, I think that's abhorrent."

She eyed the contract lying on the table between them, then wrote out her check and handed it to him. "The flower spray will cover that scratch, and with this two-thousand-dollar saving, I'm going to give a memorial to our church, I think. Something that could have a plaque on it with Robert's name."

"A wonderful idea, Mrs. Mendoz. He would have been pleased, I'm sure." Gene stood and offered his hand, then clasped hers warmly. "This will be a beautiful, beautiful service."

She gave him a watery smile. "Thank you so much."

He escorted her to the front door, offering condolences and reassurances about the arrangements she'd made for the funeral tomorrow, then smiled as he headed up to his second-floor office.

The business was so unpredictable in a small town. There might be a week or two with nothing, then several funerals could come up, just like that. So far, it had been a banner month—two funerals already in the first full week of May, and the other three homes were doing well, too.

And so was his…careful…bookkeeping.

Louise met him in the hallway upstairs. "Mrs. Mendoz is such a dear. How did it go?"

"Holding up very well. Bob was quite a bastard—she'll be a lot happier with the insurance settlement than she was with him."

"She certainly went all the way with the arrangements. The flowers alone were nearly two thousand. Orchids, roses—very specific about shade, too."

"It's all documented carefully?"

"Of course. We've also had over twenty orders for floral arrangements." Louise winked at him. "I'll be here overtime, today and tomorrow."

"As soon as he died, I placed an extra wholesale order that should arrive this afternoon. Check it over and let me know what else you need."

Louise stepped into her office, retrieved a stack of documents, came back and handed them to him. "Here are copies of the orders so far. I'm going to the basement to get started."

"Thanks." He thumbed through the orders on the way to his office, mentally calculating the volume and type of flowers to buy and then doubling that amount for expected "waste."

At his desk, he pulled up his list of floral suppliers on the computer. Who had he called last time? He snickered, in view of how little that mattered, then dialed the final number on the list.

It was all so easy. He never should have worried when he first took over the business end of things. All along, he'd been a little intimidated by Oren's successful management of the four-home chain, but what did it take? A quick mind and a sharp eye for opportunity. Oren had been weak, greedy and careless, and had too easily fallen for temptation. *Which,* Gene thought smugly to himself, *I'll never do.*

When the phone rang, he picked it up with a rush of anticipation. A banner month, indeed.

He expected to hear notification about someone newly deceased. His stomach shifted when he heard the voice on the line.

"We got a call at this number." The voice was low, laced with venom. "A hang-up, around midnight Wednesday. Was that you?"

No one used the number but him. He'd been told no one else even knew it.

"M-maybe someone misdialed."

"If someone got it from you and was checkin' us out, you're gonna be in a hell of a lot of trouble. Maybe I need to come out for a little visit."

"No! I mean, maybe I...um...hit the speed dial by accident."

"It wasn't dialed from your place. The boss *Tom* ain't happy, so now he's keeping an eye on you."

The connection clicked off. A wave of nausea crested at the back of Gene's throat.

He knew all too well what that threat could mean.

CHAPTER ELEVEN

SATURDAY DAWNED COOL and bright, with a china-blue sky and a light breeze that brought with it the scent of the mountains and newly mown grass.

"Quiet morning," Joe said to Abby over his cup of coffee. "Is everyone gone?"

He'd just finished mowing. He smelled of fresh air and faint woodsy aftershave, and Abby had to force herself to look out the window instead of at him. There was something way too appealing about those faded, soft-worn jeans that molded to his slender hips and muscular thighs, and that oxford shirt, with its open collar and rolled-back sleeves.

"Catherine got a call this morning—her niece Mandy had a C-section last night. She's gone off to Casper to help out with the older kids for a few days because Mandy's mom has the flu. Fred is working, and Sue took her daughter along to help measure the windows at her new place."

"And you?"

"Off to the library."

His voice was deep, and dark, and intensely masculine, and made her remember the moment she'd surprised herself by kissing him—her, the repressed, studious widow who'd declined every date offered to her since Oren died. *What* had she been thinking?

Not with her head, certainly.

"I might take Megan up into the foothills. I hear there are some nice trails thirty miles west of here."

"It's beautiful up there," she said wistfully. "It's been years since I've gone."

He shot her a lazy grin, beguiling as the devil. "Why don't you and Hamlet come along."

Oh, it sounded tempting. She'd been trying to ignore the growing undercurrent of sexual tension between them, and spending the day with him wouldn't help. But with Megan and Buffy along, his invitation could simply be fun—an innocent, carefree jaunt. How long had it been since she'd done anything for fun?

"I can't," she said at last. "I've got one week until finals start, and this paper has to be done by Monday morning. And poor old Hamlet wouldn't make it a half mile down the trail."

"Okay, leave him home. We'll only be gone half the day. Thirty minutes there, thirty back— and a couple hours on some easy trails."

"Well…"

"Okay—I'll drive twice as fast, and we can *run* the trails."

She burst out laughing. "I can just see that—with Buffy and Megan trying to keep up."

"Then you'll come along, and make sure I don't leave anyone behind?"

He looked so hopeful, so boyish, that her resolve melted away, and an hour later she found herself in a small meadow by a shallow stream, with Megan and the puppy racing around and a bucket of chicken from the Chicken Shack next to her on an old quilt.

"Good idea," she teased. "Consume eight thousand calories and burn roughly a hundred. The math is not in my best interest."

They'd walked a mile up the trail, until Buffy sat down and refused to go any farther. Megan's promise to carry him had lasted less than a hundred yards more.

"I'm just glad to be up here. What could be better?"

Abby had watched him while they hiked, and he seemed to take in everything—studying each new vista, each rocky outcropping and delicate wildflower, as if he'd never seen anything as beautiful. Oren would have complained about his shoes, his knees and the warm sun, and would have lasted all of twenty minutes before turning for home in a huff.

"You've never told me much about yourself," she said idly, leaning back onto her elbows. "Now you get to tell me everything, since I agreed to come along."

"I tried college, went into the marines…then came home and got married. That didn't last too long, and when Sheri and her new husband moved away with Megan…I just decided to see the country." He gave her a wry smile.

"What did you tell me once? Marriage isn't what you expect, and soon you're left with just pieces of the dream."

"Something like that." Abby toed off her sneakers and socks, and wiggled her toes. "Tell me about your wife—was she pretty?"

"That doesn't really matter in the long run, but yeah, she was."

A handsome young man, a beautiful young wife…the image filled Abby with the same faint melancholy that washed through her when she finished a good romance novel. Others found happiness with someone they loved deeply, but she never had and it wasn't likely now. She'd grown far too independent to put up with control-issue nonsense ever again. Still…

Abby sighed. "Makes you wonder, doesn't it? Look at Fred and Catherine—they're still not talking right now, but you get the feeling they must have had something once, a real spark. And yet they never got together. Some of us try, and fail. How realistic is it to ever hope for something solid and authentic with another person? Four years of social work in college, and I *still* need an attitude adjustment.''

From over by the stream came Megan's delighted laughter as Buffy pounced into the stream after a stick she'd thrown. He retrieved it, but instead of bringing it back to her, he came at a dead run for the picnic blanket, where he dropped the twig and shook furiously, spraying water over both of them.

With a gasp, Abby jumped to her feet. ''It's like ice!''

Joe stood and dried himself off, then bent to pick up the stick and throw it toward Megan. The pup took off like a golden rocket in pursuit.

The hint of sadness in his eyes as he watched his daughter and her puppy touched Abby. ''Are you still taking Megan to your brother's place when you leave here? She seems so happy now.''

He picked up the picnic litter at his feet and stowed it in the plastic sack from the restaurant. ''She'll have Buffy, and she'll be better off there.''

''But what does she *want?*''

''She lived with them three years, Abby. Maybe she's having fun right now, but what about all the times a girl really needs a mom? I can't give her that.''

"But—"

"You said you needed to be back by one o'clock," he said heavily, not meeting her eyes. "We'd better get moving."

They'd gathered everything and hiked a mile down the hill when Abby's cell phone rang. Sue's quiet, breathy voice was difficult to hear over the rush of wind in the treetops and the gurgling water of the stream, but the message was no less of a shock.

"What's wrong?" Megan demanded, tugging at her sleeve.

Numb, Abby lifted her gaze to meet Joe's. "It's Fred. He's had a heart attack, and they aren't sure if he'll make it. He's asking for me."

JOE DROVE TEN MILES over the speed limit, his attention fastened on the winding road ahead, but from the corner of his eye he could see Abby's pale, drawn face.

"He's a tough old coot, Abby. He'll pull through this and be back to taunting Catherine in no time."

"I don't know." She stared blindly out the window. "Why would he be asking for me? Maybe he has a premonition. I just feel so bad…"

"If anything happens, it's sure not your fault. He's had a good long life, independent and cantankerous to the end."

"Did you know that he has no family, other than a daughter? She tried for years to get him out of his dilapidated trailer...wanted him in residential care. If he's weakened by this, she may just put him in a nursing home."

Joe reached over and held her hand. "He'd need to be evaluated, though. With insurance and Medicare regulations, he could only get in if he truly needed the services."

"I know...I just don't want to see him change, I guess." She squeezed Joe's hand. "He's become sort of like my lovable, grumpy uncle."

They made it to the small community hospital in twenty minutes, after dropping Megan off with Sue. A nurse allowed them briefly into the ICU, where a forest of monitors and screens surrounded the head of Fred's bed, with lines and tubes and wires snaking everywhere.

The discordant beeping of monitors throughout the ICU and the whoosh of a nearby respirator were barely audible over the sound of hurried voices and the rattling of equipment.

If he'd had to guess, Joe wouldn't have laid good odds on the old guy's survival. He was lying lifelessly on the bed with the blanket drawn up to his chest. His arms and hands had already taken on a waxy hue and his face was gray.

"Hi, there," Abby whispered near Fred's ear,

cradling one of his hands within both of hers. "We sure didn't expect this."

His eyes slowly opened. "I'll be out of here soon enough," he wheezed. Out of breath from the effort, he closed his eyes and settled deeper into the pillow.

"The nurse says that they've already called your daughter. She'll be on her way as soon as she can catch a flight."

"No...need."

"We're here, though—Joe, too. If there's anything you need, we'll take care of it."

Fred lay quietly for so long that Joe glanced up at the monitors for reassurance.

"Don't...count me dead...yet," Fred whispered. "But if...I go, do two things."

"Anything," Abby said, laying a gentle hand on his forehead. "But I know you'll be back on your feet in no time. I usually have a gut feeling about these things, and I'm *never* wrong."

He took a couple of slow breaths. "Tell Catherine...she missed...the boat. Too stubborn...to see it."

Abby chuckled softly. "I'll make sure she knows."

The nurse returned, one hand on the divider sectioning off Fred's area.

"You need to go now," she said firmly. "Visits are five minutes max."

"Wait." He pulled himself up a few inches, and his voice took on a faint, desperate tone. "I—I know the…funeral home…is a Hilliard…but…" He coughed weakly. "I don't want…to go there. Gene…is…"

He fell back against the pillow, his eyes closed. The lines on the monitor jumped erratically. Leveled out. A piercing, incessant alarm sounded, even as the monitor lines began weakly squiggling across the screen once more.

"Leave, *now!*" The nurse barked, jerking the curtain back.

Joe grabbed Abby's arm as a slew of staff people hurried into the small space. "He'll be okay," he whispered in her ear as they moved quickly out of the way. "Did you see the monitor?"

They stepped outside the ICU and waited on a couple of hard plastic chairs for over an hour, until a nurse came out with a sack lunch in her hand. Abby shot to her feet. "Is Fred Wilson okay?"

The nurse's gaze flicked between Abby and Joe. "Are you family?"

"No, but—"

"I'm sorry—Federal HIPAA rules about privacy. We can't discuss anything with you unless you're his family."

"Just tell us," Joe asked quietly. "Did he make it?"

The nurse hesitated, then nodded as she scurried away.

Abby sank against Joe's chest and sighed with relief as she wrapped her arms around his waist. "Thank God."

It felt so right, having her soft warmth snuggled against him. He curved his arms around her and drew her closer, breathing in the flowery perfume of her shampoo in her baby-soft, wavy hair.

He drew back enough to kiss the top of her head, and then held her until she finally stepped away.

AT HOME, Joe watched Abby fret as she dialed Fred's daughter, Connie, to ask about his condition. The activities next door also caught his attention.

"Any idea about what's going on at the Sheltering Pines?" he asked Sue as she walked into the kitchen.

"Funeral, I suppose," she said as she reached for a box of tea bags in the cupboard. "I think the newspaper said it was for Robert Mendoz."

"A shame. A friend or relative of anyone here?"

Sue gave a wry laugh. "Only if we'd belonged to the country-club set—they hang out together and interbreed, sort of like royalty. But don't," she added darkly, "repeat what I said. I think most of the library-board members run in those circles, and I need my job.''

"I swear." He moved to the kitchen window and lifted back the lacy curtain. From this angle, he could see the tops of the cars parked behind the funeral home, but not much more. "Looks like a big crowd. Must have been quite an affair.''

"Mendoz family?" Abby nodded as she hung up the phone. "They would have had what Oren always called a KJ funeral—or 'keeping up with the Joneses.' They are always being photographed for the society news—such as it is—in the local paper.''

"I still have quite a bit of exterior painting to do over there, but this would be a late start—especially if the funeral crowd stays around.''

Sue glanced at the clock. "Usually the service takes an hour, then there's the long, slow procession to the cemetery, then the crowd goes to one of the church basements for a luncheon. I'd guess those cars over there belong to the relatives who've come back after the meal to pick up the flowers for distribution to nursing homes, and so on.''

"Guess I'll go over and check on what I still have to do. Maybe I can get a good start tomorrow morning.''

A reasonable enough excuse, he decided as he sauntered out the back door and headed for the brick wall. By the time he got there, only one car was left in the back parking lot. A 2004 Lincoln, with vanity plates reading GOLFSGR8.

A slender woman with elegantly upswept hair and a trim suit came out of the building just as he reached the wall. "Are you Mrs. Mendoz?" he called.

She glanced around in apparent confusion until she spied Joe leaning over the wall. "Yes, I am."

"I'm awfully sorry about your loss."

She gave a slight, gracious nod of her head. "I appreciate that."

"I know this is probably a bad time, but can I ask you a question?"

She hesitated, the keys jingling in her hand, then turned more fully toward him. "What?"

"I'm thinking about paying into a long-term funeral plan over there. Were you satisfied with the services?"

Her expression warmed. "Of course, this was a dreadful circumstance, but I must say—yes indeed."

"So Mr. Hilliard is a decent fellow to work with?"

"Decent? My, yes. After I paid for the casket, he found a tiny flaw. He called the company to get credit on it, then gave me a two-thousand-dollar discount. I never would have known if he hadn't pointed out the problem."

"Wow—he gave you a *refund?*"

"No, I just wrote out my check for less. Not many businessmen would have done that."

"You're absolutely right." *And especially not for the same reason.* "Sorry to have bothered you, Mrs. Mendoz."

She waved away his apology. "I'm happy to make the recommendation. I've heard such good things about that dear man from my friends, and now I know it's all true."

So Gene probably had been continuing the family business, just as Joe had suspected.

He could write an invoice for more than he actually intended to collect from a client—say, an inflated invoice for ten grand. Then he could claim to have made an "error" and collect maybe seven grand from the client—which would make the client happy—but then deposit that amount plus another three thousand of drug money that needed to look legit. The accounting books would balance with the original paperwork, the customer would be happy, and no one would be the wiser.

There were dozens of ways dirty money could be filtered into a mostly cash-based operation, especially a family-run business offering goods and services like this one. Even more so because Gene was dealing with grief-stricken people faced with huge funeral expenses, who wouldn't likely question his "good will."

Over a month's time, Gene's little laundry business—with four funeral homes under his direction—could clean a lot of money for his cohorts, between the funeral and embalming services. Add that to what might take place with the flowers and purchasing of supplies, and Gene could be a greater success under the table than he'd ever been in view of the IRS.

A sense of satisfaction swept through him as he strolled back to Abby's house.

It had taken a while, but everything was falling into place. He now had someone who'd been an unwitting partner in the scheme, he had some contact names and numbers to investigate, and somewhere in that funeral home were the documents he needed.

Just a little more time, a little more luck, a little more perseverance, and he'd have the evidence to prove his innocence. And when that happened, the people responsible for his years in hell were going to pay.

CHAPTER TWELVE

FOR ABBY the next week passed in a blur of long nights at the library researching term papers and studying for finals, and twice-daily trips to see Fred at the hospital.

His daughter had flown in and stayed for three days at his bedside. He'd shown some improvement, despite his refusal to consider surgery, and she'd had to leave for a real-estate closing, so Fred signed release papers allowing Abby to be informed about his condition.

Being busy was a good thing because it kept Abby's mind off her compelling, enigmatic boarder... a man who could make her shiver with just a smile, yet so obviously harbored secrets and a past that he didn't intend to share.

His offhand story about an unexciting, ordinary life just didn't ring true. A man who exuded that kind of confidence and control, a man who was in that sort of physical condition, couldn't have simply been aimlessly wandering the country for the past several years.

Now she stood at Fred's bedside for the second time today, with Joe at her side. The IV stands and oxygen tubing were still in place.

"How are you doing? You look better every day, far as I can tell."

Fred grunted.

"Good news! Catherine just got back to town. She's on her way over here right now."

"Tell her to go home."

Abby exchanged glances with Joe, then rested a hand on Fred's arm. "I thought you'd be happy to see her."

"Hmmph."

"She was off helping out her niece Mandy, remember? She's been calling me every day to ask about you, though."

"No point," he growled.

Footsteps came down the hall, slowed, and stopped at the door. "What's this I hear about you refusing surgery, you old coot?" Catherine strode to his bedside and glared down at him as if he were a noisy child in her library.

"Are you *crazy?*"

He didn't open his eyes. "Nice of you to stop in, Cathy."

For all of her bluster, there was deep concern etched in her face when she leaned over and brushed at his thinning hair with a gentle hand.

"My God, Frederick. A triple bypass, and you told them *no?*"

"I…couldn't…take the chance."

She gave an exasperated snort. "And what chance is that—the one giving you a full life again?"

He opened his eyes and looked up into her face with a faint smile. "The fifty-fifty chance of not surviving the surgery. I had…to stick around to see you."

"Good grief. When did that ever matter?"

Joe reached over and squeezed Abby's hand. "Maybe it's time for us to go," he whispered, leaning close to her ear.

Fred, who'd apparently feigned hearing loss for most of his days in the hospital and had seldom answered anyone, pulled himself up on one elbow.

"*Stay.* I want witnesses. Just in case ole Cathy here doesn't remember."

Catherine's back stiffened. "You haven't changed a bit. Here I was worried about you—wanting to get back as soon as I could—"

"Why?"

"Well—because." Flustered, she drew back, a hand at her chest. "We're friends."

"No, we aren't."

Speechless, she took another step back as bright spots of color swept up her wrinkled cheeks.

His skin ashen from the exertion, he dropped back against the pillow and drew in a few long breaths from the oxygen prongs at his nose. "There's always been a lot more between us... from the time you got your drawers in a twist back in high school. Over fifty years—and you've been too stubborn and stuck-up to see what's in front of your eyes."

"You got *married,*" she snapped.

"Long after I gave up on you." He took another long breath. "And I was sorry, 'cause Belle... deserved more love than I could give."

Catherine stared down at him, her mouth trembling.

"But now—I'm just plain tired of the bickering between you and me."

"I never—"

He gave a weak, impatient wave of the hand not tethered to the IV. "The hell you don't...and I'm just as bad."

"You're right," she said sadly.

"You aren't the town librarian now. I'm not just some lowly ranch hand. We're...two old people who've wasted too much time and don't have much of it left."

A burly male nurse stepped into the room. "Gotta go, folks. I need to take Mr. Wilson down for some more tests."

Fred opened his eyes and glared at him. "Not yet." He rolled his head back to face Catherine. "So what do you say—truce? A new start?" He chortled softly. "A hot date on Saturday night?"

Abby felt tears well up in her eyes as the older woman bent awkwardly over the bed and took Fred's hands, then brushed a kiss against his forehead. She tugged at Joe's arm and left the room to allow them privacy. Outside, she leaned against the wall. "That's so sweet…and so awfully sad. They could have had a lifetime together."

Joe gave her a quick hug, then draped an arm over her shoulders as they headed down the hall toward the exit. "Maybe not. Maybe until now they were too different for it to ever work out."

"Still, it's too bad. All these years of bickering…"

Joe chuckled. "Maybe for them it was sort of like polishing agates."

"Agates?"

"You start off with rough stones, and tumble them on and on until the sharp edges wear down and finally you have something worth keeping."

The weight of his arm felt so strong and protective, so reassuring, that she curved her arm around him and hooked a finger in a belt loop at his other side.

Her years with Oren hadn't been good, and she

knew that passing years wouldn't have made a difference. Trying again with someone else had never seemed worth the effort and loss of independence. Until now.

There was a lot she didn't know about Joe. He didn't begin to fit her notion of the kind of steady, dependable man who'd stay around for a lifetime, yet something about him made her want to throw caution to the winds and take chances…which was exactly how she'd ended up with a guy like Oren.

But luck was with her this time—because Joe was already planning to leave.

SATISFIED WITH a good day's work done, Gene shoved his chair away from his desk and stood, laced his fingers in front of his chest and stretched.

Dusk had fallen, and through the windows came the sound of Abby's infernal basset baying outside her back door. *Probably trying to escape the teeth and persistence of that damn pup,* he muttered to himself as he reached up to pull down and lock the lower window sash. Cats were queenly. Self-possessed. Dogs—he shuddered, thinking about paw prints and drooling and how they always tried to shove their noses up his crotch.

Abby had proven as difficult after Oren's death as she'd been before, and those two obnoxious dogs were a case in point. She possessed no sense of propriety or duty, yet she'd shown an irritating knack for finding little details in the bookkeeping that didn't quite add up, and had been damn persistent with her questions. He'd stopped asking her to help in the office, but recently she'd been calling to ask questions, and sometimes stopping to check things out.

As if she has the right, he thought grimly as he closed the open programs on his computer and changed his password before shutting down for the night. *She has no idea what has to be done here.*

Since that threatening call a week ago, he'd been more careful than ever—checking each window lock on both floors of the building before he left, double-checking the door locks.

He'd starting sleeping here more often, too—the small apartment down the hall had been meant only for a night-duty person to catch a few winks if all was quiet, but he felt safer keeping a close eye on things.

He shuddered, remembering the day his contact—Tom—had first shown up, just days after Oren died. The guy had tattoos and a shaved head, and he'd been damn clear about the setup.

Cooperation meant money, and lots of it. Difficulties meant swift retribution, and there was no way to blithely say ''No thanks'' and walk away.

Tom's phone call last Friday had felt like a

plunge into ice water. How could anyone have obtained that secret phone number? No one else used Gene's computer or had access to the database where the private numbers were kept. It had to have been a simple misdial. Unless...

A door creaked downstairs.

Surprised, Gene glanced at his watch. Louise was long gone. There weren't funerals or weddings tomorrow that required her to work. And he'd *personally* locked that door behind her when she left at five.

He pursed his lips. If someone had gotten into his records before, this might be a return trip. And this time, he'd be ready.

Guns were distasteful. He'd never liked the weight of them in his hand or the feeling of such reckless power, and he'd never believed he could pull the trigger and send a bullet ripping through another person's flesh.

On the other hand, he could face a bullet himself if he allowed any interference in his business. He suppressed a shudder as he reached into his upper-right desk drawer and emptied the contents onto his desk. Papers. Boxes of staples and rubber bands. Envelopes.

The small black metal box, which he'd found in Oren's desk in the Winthrop branch of the Sheltering Pines.

He was so intent that he didn't see the man in front of him until it was too late to duck.

In one dizzying rush, he felt himself thrown against the wall. Pain exploded through him as his head hit the plaster and a knee slammed into his groin. Pictures crashed to the floor.

Nauseous, his head throbbing, he slid into a crumpled heap and stared stupidly up at the man towering over him. Heavy black biker boots. Black leathers. A black muscle shirt stretched tight over a massive chest.

A man with a shaved head and tattoos covering his arms like a severe case of mold. *Tom.*

Nausea and fear overwhelmed Gene as he struggled for consciousness. *Escape—I've got to get out of here—*

But there was only one thought that pulsed through his aching brain now, eclipsing all the rest.

This will be the day I die.

LEANING ON THE LAWN EDGER, Joe looked back at the sidewalk leading up to Abby's spacious front porch. He'd never done much yard work before—with his erratic hours and undercover assignments that sometimes kept him away from home for weeks at a time, he'd lived in apartments and condos, even after he and Sheri married.

She'd wanted a house with a picket fence.

He'd wanted a place to crash with minimal upkeep.

And since then, he'd had a lot of time to think about how he had failed her in so many ways. Failed as a husband, and a father. But with this gift of a second chance at being Megan's dad, he wasn't going to make the same mistakes. He was going to make every moment count.

The heady thrill of being outdoors, of doing whatever he wanted to do, still hit him at odd moments and nearly took his breath away. The rich smells of earth and cut grass and spring flowers were like perfume, and being tired at night after a hard day's work out of doors filled him with deep satisfaction.

Skimming off his ball cap, he shoved a hand through his hair, then resettled the cap low over his forehead. This was a beautiful old house. Out on the street, the lamps flickered on, and the crisp white trim showed up in stark contrast to the red brick.

He'd repaired shutters and fences and moldings, painted trim and worked on the overgrown shrubbery until the place practically sparkled.

Abby had hinted at plans to sell the house and move on after this summer, depending on where she found a job after she graduated. It would show better now than it would have when he arrived, and would likely bring a lot more money, but the thought filled him with more regret than satisfaction.

A home like this would be good for raising a family. Seeing your kids grow up, and your grandkids come to play. He shook his head at the thought. That wasn't likely to happen for him, here or anywhere else.

When he was done with his investigation, he cast a disparaging glance at the funeral home next door, and then did a double take. A dark car eased backward out of the driveway, not fifty feet away.

Joe dropped the garden tool he'd been holding and slipped quickly along the inside of the hedge, bending low and out of sight. The driver halted briefly at the street and Joe got a glimpse of him before he swung around with a creaking of the chassis and peeled out.

Quickly reciting the license-plate number under his breath, he searched his pockets until he found a gas station receipt and a stubby pencil, and wrote it down.

I've seen that face before. Vivid memories rocketed through his mind. The last weeks of his investigation into the Sheltering Pines funeral home in Dalton.

The day he'd gone to his car and found three

cops standing next to it, their arms folded and their faces grim.

Adrenaline surged through him as he shoved the scrap of paper into his back pocket, pivoted and retrieved the lawn edger.

Until he proved his innocence, he was just another ex-con turned back out on the street by the overloaded criminal-justice system—still the dirty DEA agent who'd gone against every code of honor and pride. *But it won't be long now.*

A soft voice behind him stopped him in his tracks.

"Is that you, Joe?" Louise stood out on the sidewalk in a pale blue jogging suit, with a Pekinese on a leash, and a curious expression on her face. She gave a silvery, flirtatious laugh. "Must be hard doing yard work in the dark."

"Just finishing up." How long had she been there? She'd have to think it odd if she'd seen him check that license plate, so he gestured vaguely toward the funeral home. "The lights are all off over there, but a car just left. You haven't had any problems with vandals, have you?"

"At a place like that? Hardly." She appeared old enough to be his mother, but he could have sworn she batted her eyelashes at him. "Then again, sometimes we have problems around Halloween."

"Do you like working there? I mean, it seems like a sad sort of place to be, day after day."

She gave a delicate shrug. "Some people can't handle it. They leave the business, or lose themselves in alcohol or drugs—like with any high-stress career."

"And the rest?"

"Most of us feel a sense of…pride, I guess. People comforted. Arrangements managed in a respectful way. It's important, and sooner or later we all need that service, right?" She eyed him. "What about you? Are you staying in these parts much longer?"

"Early June, probably."

"Will you be looking for more odd jobs in the next town?" She clucked her tongue. "A young man like you could go to school, learn a trade. Establish a future somewhere."

"I suppose…"

"Then again, it must be fun to be footloose and fancy-free. When I was a girl, I dreamed of seeing the world. I didn't get more than four hours from home, though. Sort of like your Abby, there."

A flicker of surprise rippled through him. "Abby?"

"Well, you know…she grew up in Winthrop, and lived there all her married life with Oren. Now she's here, because that house wasn't as nice as this one. There's a director's house next to each of the four funeral homes, you know.''

"She'd mentioned something like that," he said carefully.

"And that she's a half owner?" Louise chuckled. "That girl talks about moving on, but she's fully involved in the business and she isn't going anywhere. She's told me herself." Louise pressed the light-up dial of her wristwatch. "Oh, my—where does the time go? I'd better be off, or Twinkles won't get her walk in tonight. See you later."

Joe stared after her as she started down the sidewalk. She hadn't been concerned about the potential for prowlers, but she'd raised questions about Abby's involvement in the family business.

Just how deeply was Abby involved—and how much could he trust her?

CHAPTER THIRTEEN

ABBY WALKED in the back door of the house Monday afternoon, dropped her book bag on the kitchen table and gave a gusty sigh of relief. "One down, two to go," she said, heading for the refrigerator. "This was the tough one—Social Work Policies and Issues—but I cannot wait until the rest of my finals are *over*."

Catherine looked up from the bread dough she was kneading on the counter.

"You've done well, I'm sure. I don't believe you could have worked any harder."

"Where is everyone?" Abby hunted through the fruit drawer, found an apple and took it to the sink to rinse it off. "Even the dogs are quiet."

"Sue's working, the girls are in school. The dogs were barking at squirrels, so I put them down in the basement for a while. Joe…" Her forehead wrinkled. "He's been gone for a few hours. Maybe he's even upstairs by now, but I didn't see him come in."

"Fred?"

"I spent most of the morning at the hospital with him, before they transported him to the hospital in Casper." Catherine's voice wavered. "He says he's ready for his surgery, but sure isn't looking forward to it."

"Will his daughter make it back in time?"

"She called him and said she'll be flying into Casper tonight."

"I know she'll call us right away with any news." Abby hovered over the counter and breathed in the rich aroma of warm yeast, whole-wheat flour and honey. "This is *wonderful*. There's nothing on earth better than your homemade bread."

Catherine turned the mass over, gave it one last shove, then formed it into a smooth shape and dropped it into a waiting bread pan. "Takes my mind off things, I guess."

"How are things going with you two?" There were two other loaves of bread on the counter, and what looked like a pan of cinnamon rolls, all rising under clean tea towels. The clear glass cookie jar was stuffed full, so Abby had a fairly good idea.

"He thinks we ought to get *married*." The older woman raised a flustered hand to her face, smoothing several stray wisps of hair back into place. "At my age!"

"Commitment. Promises. Being together all the time. That doesn't sound too bad to me."

"People would *talk.* 'Imagine—that old spinster snagging a husband after she dried up on the vine.'"

Abby took a bite of her apple and leaned one hip against the counter. "Does it matter?"

"Yes…no…" Catherine washed her hands under the sink, scrubbing them until they were bright pink. "I've spent my life *alone,* Abigail. It's what I know. And what if…well…what if I disappointed him and ruined everything?"

"He knows you pretty well by now."

"But I'm stubborn, and arrogant, and I'm used to having my own way. A few months ago he told me it was foolish to gamble my money, and I went to the track just to rebel."

Abby hid a smile. The two had feuded over that incident for a week afterward, but Catherine hadn't gone since.

"My linens are folded just so," Catherine continued. "Dust drives me mad. What if I make the man miserable? Maybe it's better to just stay friends."

"If you put those worries aside, and just look at how you feel, deep in your heart, what do you want?"

Catherine gave a short, bitter laugh. "I want to

be twenty again. Pretty, and young, with a lifetime ahead of me for making the right choices instead of the wrong ones. A chance to marry young and have a family. Pride has been very poor company, I'm afraid.''

''Both of you are strong and independent, but you can adapt.'' When Catherine still didn't answer, Abby moved closer and rested a hand on hers. ''Remember the poster on a wall in the self-help section at the library? Golda Meir was seventy-one when she became prime minister of Israel. Grandma Moses started a wonderful career in painting at eighty.''

''And Hayakawa was elected to the U.S. Senate at seventy,'' Catherine recited as she stared out the window above the sink, her vein-gnarled hands braced on the rim of the counter. ''But those are *career* changes.''

''If you give up this chance to be with a man who loves you—even if it's a little late in the game—what will you gain?''

When Catherine finally looked over her shoulder there was a sheen in her eyes. ''Nothing. Nothing at all.''

''Sooo…''

After a long silence, Catherine's mouth curved into a soft, almost girlish smile. ''Maybe it's time

I finally gave the town gossips something to talk about. Don't set a place for me at supper—I think I'll go to Casper.''

AFTER SUPPER, Megan and Lindsey were in the backyard playing with Buffy and Hamlet when someone pounded on the front door. Joe looked up from beneath the kitchen sink, where he was fixing a leak in the garbage disposal. ''Want me to get that?''

''Probably someone trying to sell me something,'' Abby said. ''New roofs—aluminum windows—insurance—it never ends.''

At the front entry she found Mrs. Foley's grunge-rock son. She sighed and opened the door wide, wishing she could have any other neighbors in town than the Foleys. ''What's up, Curt?''

''Those damn dogs of yours—they were barking all day, and Ma's calling a lawyer on you if it happens again. Or,'' he added with a nasty gleam in his eye, ''I'll take care of them myself.''

Abby felt Joe come up behind her, but she waved him back. Curt always stood too close, using his height and size for intimidation. His unpredictable, impulsive manner that set her nerves on edge.

Now she'd had enough.

''Listen, Curt. I'm calling the sheriff and my own lawyer. That isn't a threat, it's a fact.''

He was a good six inches taller than her, and the short sleeves of his T-shirt stretched tight over his biceps and his muscular forearms folded across his chest. But Abby didn't finish.

"What do you think—should I go to court and get a restraining order against you? The local reporter doesn't have much to do around here—he'd be happy to do a story on this, and I'm sure your mother would love the publicity. Her Garden Club friends would be so impressed. But I don't imagine the local judge will be very happy to see your name come up. *Again*."

Curt glanced toward the street. She could almost see him pondering this change of events. "If our dogs cause a disturbance," she continued, "you have every right to complain—without threats to me, the people who live here, or the dogs. Is that clear enough?"

Curt gave a single nod.

"If you come to my door again, you'd better have a smile on your face. And if anything unusual happens around here, you'll be the first one the sheriff comes to visit, because he'll know all about our little differences."

Like a mouse mesmerized by a stalking cat, Curt stood frozen in place until Abby extended a hand. "Deal?"

Curt warily accepted the single handshake, then

took the steps two at a time and left at a fast jog without looking back.

"Nice job," Joe said.

"Maybe I've been learning from you. You sure handled the Cailey boys well. And," she added with a grin, "I knew you were here to back me up."

He brushed his knuckles against her cheek. "You did just fine on your own."

"Where did you get to be so good with confrontations? I remember Jason and Sam were definitely impressed."

"I was in the service." He gave a little shrug as he headed for the kitchen.

"Doing *what?*"

"The usual." He went back under the sink with a wrench in his hand. "Guess I still feel disrespect should be dealt with."

And that, she knew, would be as much as he would say.

There were dark things in his past, she was sure of it. She'd seen it in his eyes. But he was also an honorable man who made her feel safe. And just an inadvertent touch, or glance, or—God help her—his kiss had the power to fill her with such longing and need that she knew she could easily lose control.

She found herself wishing for time that didn't

exist—a chance to work past those mysterious layers to the man inside, to find out if he was all she
imagined. But he'd soon be gone, and she knew
he wouldn't be coming back.

And that thought filled her with a sense of loss.

MEGAN HAD LESS than three weeks left of the
school year, and then Joe's reasons for hanging
around town were going to seem rather thin.

Three weeks left to get the evidence he
needed—but with Gene staying at the funeral home
almost every night and the longer hours Louise
was putting in on prom and wedding flowers, there
hadn't been much chance to delve further into the
documents in Gene's office.

He'd felt his frustration grow day by day. The
license plate he'd traced a week ago had come
from the same area as a number of small Denver
businesses Gene dealt with. Was the driver coming
for legitimate business, or something else? And Joe
could have sworn that Gene had been in some sort
of altercation—he was limping and had a poorly
concealed bruise on one cheek.

Now, as Joe brushed paint on the frame of the
last cellar window of the funeral home, he weighed
his options. Calling in the local DEA wasn't one
of them—he still didn't know which of his old

buddies had set him up, and the less they all knew, the better.

He could sit down with the sheriff's department...but in a town this small, ferreting out possible connections and allegiances would take more time than he had, and if anyone in the sheriff's office was on Gene's payroll, Joe could kiss his chances goodbye.

He could risk entering at night when Gene was there, and disable the antiquated alarm system fast enough to avoid detection, but if Gene awakened, he'd probably call 911. If Joe was fingerprinted, his cover would be blown and there would never be a chance to clear his name—anyone involved would make sure every last shred of evidence was destroyed.

Or, he could take a chance and trust Abby with what he knew.

After seven weeks in Silver Springs he felt sure she'd been unaware of her late husband's activities—yet family loyalty could be strong, and he'd already seen her devotion to her boarders. He'd also seen how much she valued trust and honesty, and could well imagine her reaction when she discovered the true reasons he'd come to town.

Tugging at the window, he set it ajar to paint the edges and allow it to dry without sealing shut, then leaned farther down to inspect the back of the frame.

He settled back on his heels in surprise.

All of the basement-window glass of the old mansion had been painted black from the inside. Per regulation, Gene had explained, to keep the curious from trying to peer in on the embalming and preparation rooms. In addition to the usual screens, well-secured steel bars had been installed long ago.

There were only empty holes in this sill, and from the swathe of spiderwebs covering them, the bars had been removed a long time ago. There weren't even any security-system wires—probably ignored because the window was so small.

Joe reached for the powerful Maglite on his tool belt and swept it through the darkness inside. Maybe six-by-eight feet, the room was dusky and plain, with bare studs and grimy residue staining the walls to a height of seven or eight feet. An abandoned coal bin, probably, and not used for decades. A small door fitted with vertical pulleys stood on the opposite wall.

It would provide an entrance, one not easily detected...making it possible to search the basement and then gain access to other areas, as well.

Tonight, he was coming back.

JOE WAITED UNTIL Megan and all the others had turned in, then went outside to sit on the front porch, where he gazed at the stars and occasionally glanced at the Sheltering Pines building until all the upstairs lights went out.

After waiting an extra half hour, he slipped over the brick wall and moved through the shadows to the basement window he'd found earlier.

Before switching gears and moving to the DEA, Joe had worked his way up from street cop to homicide detective by the time he turned twenty-eight, thanks to a captain who'd thought he had potential, and a slew of department retirements that created opportunity for advancement.

During his career he'd collected evidence from medical examiners, accompanied bodies to the morgue and attended a number of autopsies, and he'd seen things that had kept him awake at night.

But those days were over, and slipping into the dark coal bin of the Sheltering Pines at midnight gave him a chill. Before, he'd done undercover work on assignment. Now, he was on his own, and the courts would hardly be impressed by an ex-con found breaking and entering within weeks of his release.

He wouldn't take anything—he couldn't use any of it for evidence without a search warrant—but knowing the presence and location of documents or other pertinent items would make contacting the authorities a far safer bet.

Arrowing a thin beam of light at the bare floor, he made his way across the room, swept the flashlight beam over the walls at closer range.

In the corner he found the door hanging on a pulley system. A slight nudge with the toe of his running shoe sent something scurrying on tiny feet on the other side.

He switched off the flashlight, lifted the door partway, then lowered himself to the dusty floor and peered into the darkness on the other side. Reassured, he eased himself through.

The door opened into the shadowy end of a linoleum-floored hallway that stretched the width of the building, with rooms on either side. A couple of low-watt lightbulbs along the ceiling and an Exit sign at the far end provided dim illumination.

He stopped and listened for a moment, then moved silently down the hallway, testing doorknobs and finding them locked. A couple of sets of double doors marked No Admittance likely led into the embalming and preparation areas. He passed an elevator. More locked doors, with only a broom closet left open. At the end he saw a stairwell.

Behind him, he heard the soft hum and creak of

a moving elevator. A faint *ding,* and the soft *whoosh* of its doors opening.

He flattened himself against the wall and slipped into the closet, pulling the door closed behind him, and prayed he wasn't about to come face-to-face with a night cleaning crew.

One doorknob after another rattled and rubber-soled shoes squeaked against the flooring as someone came down the hall checking the locks. Joe held his breath and leaned back as the footsteps pulled to a halt in front of the closet.

The knob turned.

The door opened a few inches, sending a shaft of light spearing into the closet inches away from his shoulder.

With an oath—Gene's voice, Joe realized—the man outside jangled a set of keys and locked the door, then moved on down the hall. Seconds later, hinges squealed as another door opened wide.

And then silence fell.

Minutes ticked by. Four…five…six…

So what was Gene doing in the basement after midnight? His office was up on the second floor, and the last room on the left had appeared to be just a small one, so it probably wasn't an area where he would deal with someone newly deceased.

Joe tested the doorknob and, thankful that it had

an inside release mechanism, eased the door open a few inches, then wider. A thin apron of light glowed from beneath the next door down. He moved soundlessly toward it, his muscles tense and ready.

But given the sounds coming from inside, Gene wouldn't have heard a cattle drive coming down the hall.

Cardboard boxes thudded to the floor. Joe could hear shipping tape being ripped away. Papers rustled.

Gene uttered a muffled cry of impatience, and more boxes slammed against the floor. Above it all came the cheerful jingle of a cell phone.

"What?" he snapped, then, in a calmer voice, said, "Mrs. Kelley, at the E.R. Got it. An hour all right? Okay, okay—I'm on my way. Fifteen minutes, tops."

Apparently he had a pickup to do…and soon would be back down here with a body. Joe slipped into the closet until Gene hurried by on the way to the elevator.

When he was gone, Joe checked out the room Gene had been in. In his haste, the guy had left the door wide open, and inside there was a tumble of storage boxes on the floor and papers stacked in haphazard heaps. Other boxes filled the shelves lining the walls. Some clearly were file storage boxes, marked by year and month. Others were unlabeled and anybody's guess.

Joe stepped farther into the room and bent to shuffle through the loose papers. Receipts. Invoices. Correspondence.

Something had frightened Gene enough to have him frantically searching for…what? Documents involving his money-laundering activities, probably. Receipts, canceled checks and bank statements that didn't match up. Old funeral-service contracts.

Joe smiled. He'd arrived with perfect timing, because that's what he was after, as well, and now he knew where to start looking.

He took one last look around the room, then headed down the hallway to exit the same way he'd arrived.

It was time to leave, but Joe definitely planned to be back.

CHAPTER FOURTEEN

"IT WAS SO NICE of you to help us move Sue and Lindsey today." Abby stretched her tired muscles, then peeled off the work gloves she'd worn and tossed them on the settee as she walked down the hall to the kitchen. "It would have taken twice as long otherwise."

"Not a problem." Joe tossed his own gloves next to hers. "With the rental truck it only took two trips."

"Plus all the packing, and unpacking, and cleaning up."

Joe and Megan followed her into the kitchen, where she shook some chocolate cookies from the jar onto a plate and pulled a gallon of milk from the fridge.

"I'm gonna miss Lindsey," Megan said. "Even if she is only a few blocks away."

"And she'll miss you, too. I think that's why they invited you for a sleepover tonight." Abby gave her a reassuring hug as she handed her a glass of milk. "But you two will still be seeing each other every day at school, and Aimee often comes over after school. Now that the weather is getting warmer, you girls will have lots of fun on that water slide your dad bought you. He got you some books, too, didn't he?''

''Oh, gosh—I think I left them out in his car yesterday, and I want to take one over to Lindsey's.'' Megan set her cookies and milk aside and disappeared out the back door, then popped back in. ''I'll pack quick, and then you can walk me back to Lindsey's, right?''

''If you want me to.'' Joe frowned as he watched her leave. ''I wonder if this is a good night for her to go over there. Sue must be tired, and the girls, too. They helped quite a bit.''

''Spoken like a good dad,'' Abby said lightly. ''It's up to you—though I think the girls are counting on camping under blanket tents in Sue's living room.''

''I think that—''

The back screen door crashed against the porch railing as Megan raced in.

''Dad! It's your *car!*''

Joe stood and caught her shoulders as she breathlessly rushed up to him.

''What's wrong? Are you okay?''

''There's a broken window, and headlight, and someone put a dent in the hood. It's *awful!*''

Abby spun toward the windows and scanned the scene. Rosy, early-evening light bathed the garage in pink, and inside the fenced backyard, both Hamlet and Buffy were flopped in the grass, sleeping.

They'd probably watched the vandals with mild interest, their tails wagging with hope for a doggie treat, then curled up for a nap in disappointment. The only "intruders" they ever barked at were squirrels, blackbirds and Mrs. Foley's cat.

Abby wrapped her arms around her waist and shivered. "I'll call the police."

"Wait." Joe gave Megan a hug. "I want to do a sweep of the house first. You two stay right here in the kitchen, and don't touch anything."

In a small town like this one, people seldom locked their doors, and hers had been open all day while they were helping Sue. An image of some burglar hiding upstairs and leaping out to attack him sent a rush of icy fear through Abby's veins…yet she'd seen Joe in action before, and this time she would trust him.

Still, the minutes ticked by so slowly that she was ready to make that 911 call, anyway, when she heard him come down the stairs.

"Nothing has been disturbed as far as I can tell—drawers are all shut, nothing has been disarrayed. The DVD and VCR are still in the parlor…and I saw a laptop and camera sitting out on your desk, Abby. You might want to check your jewelry and other valuables, though.'' He briefly rested a hand on Megan's shoulder and headed for the back door. "I'll go look around outside.''

"What if they'd hurt Buffy or Hamlet—or come in the house and kidnapped us, or something?'' Megan shuddered. "Like the stuff that happens on the news?''

"The dogs looked perfectly content, and your dad would have protected us very well, don't you think?'' Abby tried for her most nonchalant smile, though Megan had just echoed her own thoughts. *What if…*

"Let's just finish our milk and cookies, okay? When Joe comes in we'll take you to Lindsey's, if you still want to go.''

Megan flicked a nervous glance at the windows. "Do you think I should?''

"Everything will be fine here. I promise.''

"But my dad…what if something *happens* to him?''

"He's a very strong man, and knows how to take care of himself. Remember the day you came here? He handled those bad guys at that filling station, easy as could be. Didn't even have a scratch, did he?'' Over Megan's shoulder, Abby saw Joe come back into the kitchen, and she raised an eyebrow at him. "Nothing will happen to your dad, sweetie."

Megan's lower lip trembled. "I just have a bad feeling that something will."

"The house was untouched, Megan." He crossed the room and bent to cradle her face in both hands. "Everything outside is fine except my Blazer—and I have a few good ideas about who could have done the damage. You don't need to worry, believe me."

Standing near him, sensing his calm, absolute confidence, Abby felt her own fears slip away. "The Cailey boys again? Or Curt Foley?"

He met her gaze. "Maybe."

"Are you reporting this, then?"

"I'll need to, for insurance purposes, but it can be done tomorrow." He poured a glass of milk and gave it to Abby, then poured one for himself.

"I'd rather enjoy some of these good cookies right now, wouldn't you? Then I'll help Megan pack and take her to Lindsey's."

A half hour later, Abby watched Joe and his daughter walk out the front door, with Megan's hand held firmly in his, and her glittery pink backpack slung over his other shoulder. Abby smiled, even as a melancholy feeling settled over her.

She'd wanted children so much, but it had never happened. Her fertility tests had been inconclusive and Oren had refused to risk his pride, so they'd bumped along one year after another, until they were soon no more than two strangers in a cold house.

Seeing Joe's earnest efforts at becoming a father touched her. And tonight, after he'd seen the damage to his SUV, he'd shown none of the rage she would have expected from Oren. Instead, he'd handled the situation with his usual calm and level-headed manner.

His ex-wife had to have been crazy to walk away from a man like Joe…and if he married in the future, his new wife would be the luckiest woman alive.

Abby shut the front door and locked it, then leaned against it and closed her eyes as she accepted the emotions that had been flickering inside her for the past few weeks. She hadn't known him long, but some things were almost meant to be…a connection, a sort of chemistry that happened without intent or even awareness, until it was too late.

When Joe left Silver Springs in a few weeks, he would be taking a big piece of her heart.

"I DON'T KNOW why you came all this way," Fred grumbled. "My daughter will be here in a couple of hours."

Catherine gave a nonchalant flip of a hand.

"Nothing better to do, I guess." He looked so gray and weak, lying in that hospital bed, that she wished she could slip under the covers and just hold him close.

His forehead furrowed. "How in tarnation did you get here?"

"I borrowed Sue's car." She allowed herself a smug smile, wanting the reassurance of their old verbal sparring in this cold place smelling of antiseptic and crisp linens. "I do know how to drive, you know, and I've not had a single ticket in over sixty years behind the wheel."

"I've *seen* you drive. I'm sure the cops are all afraid to get too close."

"They know better than to tamper with perfection." She tried to stifle her thoughts as she pulled a chair close to his bed. By this time tomorrow, the surgery would be over—and fifty-fifty odds didn't sound good. "And they probably couldn't have caught up with me, because I knew I had to get here tonight."

"What, you think I'll kick the bucket?" Fred's laughter was rusty.

The thought wrapped around her heart like an icy hand. "Of course not, you old goat. You're too ornery to die."

His smile faded and his gaze met hers, intense. Searching. "Then why are you here?"

The words came hard.

Back when they were young, she'd been certain that he would come back to her after their last big fight. When he left town for a while and then married someone else, she'd found comfort in self-righteous anger at his betrayal. That anger built walls around her that no one had ever breached.

"I...came to apologize." She clenched her hands together in her lap. "And to collect on something you owe me."

"Apologize?" he wheezed. "You? Now I *know* the world is going to end."

"I'm not joking anymore." She leaned forward and held his hand, ignoring the tears burning beneath her eyelids. "I pushed you into agreeing to this surgery. Now I'm so afraid—maybe you were right, not wanting to go ahead."

He closed his eyes and inhaled on the oxygen cannula prongs in his nose.

"It wasn't a choice if I want to see my grandchild grow up. You gave me the courage to do it. Though I've gotta admit, I wouldn't mind riding out of here on a good horse right now."

A nurse bustled into the room and hung some new bags of IV fluid, gave him some pills and checked his blood pressure.

When she was gone, Fred rolled his head against the pillow to face Catherine once again. "I think she gave me a sleeper, so you'd better tell me what I owe you before I doze off.''

"The hot date. Remember? You asked me while you were in the Silver Springs hospital, and now I've come to collect.''

He laughed softly. "Guess it might be a while now. Wouldn't you know—my big chance with the prettiest gal in town, and I'm trapped in this bed.''

"I'm considering this our hot date,'' she said. "I'll be here until your surgery, and I'll be here when you wake up. We can always do something a little wilder later. Deal?''

He held her gaze with his own as he brushed a kiss against her hand.

"Deal.''

Relief…and joy…and the beginnings of something much deeper eased through her, and though she was sitting in a hospital room filled with a jumble of high-tech equipment, Catherine felt as if she'd finally come home.

AFTER CHECKING all the doors, Abby rambled around the empty house for a while, picking up books and setting them down, blowing dust from the curios she hadn't had time to clean during the last few weeks of spring semester. Finally, still feeling restless, she drew a deep, hot bubble bath and leaned back to immerse herself up to her chin.

With finals done and her term papers completed, time suddenly seemed to stretch like a great void until summer school started. Catherine would be bringing Fred home from the hospital tomorrow, though, and then the rest of her substitute family would be back together.

How did people ever manage living alone? She loved noise, and confusion, and togetherness. She'd once dreamed of having children—four or five—with all of their pets and friends filling her house, and she'd dreamed of having a truly loving marriage, too. Which just went to prove that dreams were a waste of time.

She dressed in a set of purple velour sweats and towel dried her hair, then went downstairs to curl up on the sofa in the parlor to contemplate the possibilities.

The fridge needed cleaning.

Hamlet needed a bath—no, wait. Wrong timing, if she'd just had a nice bath of her own. Any dirt on him invariably ended up on *her*.

A stack of to-be-read paperbacks was waiting by her bed, because she hadn't had time to read for pleasure all semester.

And then there was Louise, who often stopped by for coffee or just to chat when she happened to see Abby in the front yard. She always talked about how much she'd like to go to the movies, but the seven o'clock show had to be almost over by now.

Still edgy, Abby hit the TV remote and flipped through all three channels available in Silver Springs without cable, then hit the Off button and headed for the kitchen. *Cookies*. Maybe she just needed a few more cookies.

Or maybe just a whole new life.

Going through the kitchen door she ran into Joe, who was leaving with a few cookies of his own.

Running into him—literally—was like hitting a wall. "I'm sorry," she murmured, feeling foolish and awkward, and more than a little embarrassed.

"I didn't realize you were back."

"I had to stay and help build a fortress," he admitted as he stepped aside to let her pass. "Sue's living room is chaos, but the girls are happy."

"I'll bet they are." Abby moved past him and opened the back door to let Buffy and Hamlet in for the night. Hamlet ambled in with a look of sorrow on his droopy face. Buffy romped in after him, bounced against Abby's legs, then took off like a shot in search of something to fetch.

A second later he came back into the kitchen, his tail wagging and a candle—unlit, fortunately— in his teeth.

"I think that was on an end table, Buffy," she

said, gently prying it from the puppy's mouth. "Why don't you fetch a ball or a newspaper?"

"He probably knows he'll get more attention." Joe reached down to rub the pup behind his ears. "It sure is quiet around here."

"Strange, isn't it? Right now it feels so empty that the house just sort of echoes." She reached for the container of dog biscuits on the counter and tossed one to each dog. "Honestly, I'm glad you're back."

"Did you have a chance to check your things?"

The reminder made her shiver. "Just a quick look—but so far I can't find anything gone. How bad is your car?"

"Offhand, I'd guess maybe a thousand dollars' damage, though I haven't had any bodywork done in a long time. Could be more."

She grabbed a cookie and hopped up on the counter instead of taking it to the kitchen table. "You were sort of vague earlier. Who did it, do you think?"

"Not those two boys, and probably not Curt, either. This took a lot of power, and it took a lot of rage. I can't see any of them working that hard to make a point."

"Or being foolish enough to cross you again. Which leaves…"

"Someone wanting to send me a message. Who, I couldn't say."

Or doesn't want to. "Some message. Have you made any enemies in Silver Springs? Broken any hearts? Courted any ladies with jealous boyfriends?"

"I'm not quite *that* careless."

The rich baritone vibration of his laughter sensitized her skin, warming her and making her much too aware of him as not just another boarder, but as an intensely masculine, powerful and compelling man. One who well exceeded any fantasy she'd ever had.

The air between them changed.

Heated.

His gaze drifted lower and settled on her mouth, then lifted, and they stared at each other for a moment.

"I think," he said finally, his voice laced with regret, "that I should go upstairs and turn in."

"Probably."

"Anything more would just create complications."

"True." But the unexpected hint of wistfulness in his eyes kept her from moving away. *It had been so long, so very long…and the thought that it might have been the same for him made her pulse leap at her wrists.*

He stepped closer. "Well…maybe just this."

He brushed a kiss against her mouth.

"Or this."

He reached up and cupped a hand behind her head, then curved an arm behind her shoulders and pulled her into the most dizzying, electrifying kiss of her life. He was at once tender and possessive, exploring her mouth with such focus that she felt as if she was at the center of the universe.

When he pulled back, his eyes were dark and searching. "You are," he said after a long silence, "the most incredible woman on this planet."

The moment his mouth left hers she felt empty, aching and needy. He'd be leaving soon. She knew he wouldn't be back. But she also knew that to miss this chance would mean that she might live with regret forever.

"And this," she said slowly, "might just be the chance of a lifetime. You and me—here alone."

"You're sure?" He took a step back, clearly offering her space to refuse.

"No second thoughts?"

Maybe there would be, but for once in her life she wanted to be loved. Held. Cherished. "None at all."

His gaze burned into hers as his slow grin filled with wicked promise.

One moment, she was still perched on the edge

of the cabinet. The next, she was swept away in a dizzying rush as he lifted her into his arms.

"Where?" he growled.

Disoriented and giddy, feeling more reckless and excited than she'd ever felt before, she wrapped her arms around his neck and kissed his cheek. "The roof. Definitely, the roof."

ABBY EASED UP on one elbow and gently pulled the covers up over Joe's shoulders, then stared at the dark sweep of lashes resting against his high, tanned cheekbones and the wavy dark hair that curled over his forehead. Even in sleep he was so beautiful that her heart ached.

They'd gone to the roof—a covered widow's walk where they'd piled blankets and pillows and made love in the cool night air. And then there'd been the parlor. The living room.

And finally, Abby's room up under the eaves, where they'd collapsed into exhausted sleep, and she'd dreamed of Joe at forty, fifty, seventy—living here, loving her until they were both gray and bent with arthritis.

The dreams were better than the waking.

She'd slept with her late husband—at least in the early years. Joe had made *love* to her.

The difference was so vast, so unbelievable, that she felt her eyes burn with sudden tears at how much she'd missed in her life without ever knowing. And now, in a few short weeks, Joe would be gone, leaving her with only the memories…love and longing that she would carry until the day she died. But surely that would be better than never having known him at all.

Not wanting the night to end, she dropped back to her pillow and closed her eyes.

JOE HAD ALWAYS been a light sleeper.

In prison, he'd learned to be constantly on his guard. When his cellmate had been pulled out for solitary and he was alone, he'd awakened at the slightest noise—a fact that had saved his life twice. For an ex-agent or ex-cop, prison could be deadly.

So now, even after the most incredible night he could remember, he dozed with his arm draped around Abby and her back snuggled firmly against his chest, but he still was aware of the first glimmer of dawn outside her lacy curtains.

The moment she'd awakened, then dropped back to sleep.

The digital clock that read 5:13 a.m.

The creaks of an old house settling in for another day.

And then, another distant sound that didn't belong. A jiggle of a lock. And again…like the scrabble of mice…or someone using a scrubbing motion with tools for picking a lock.

Fully alert now, he eased his arm away from Abby and soundlessly rose to his feet. With his clothes strewn somewhere downstairs, he grabbed a towel from her bathroom and knotted it securely around his waist, then crept down the steep flight of stairs to the second floor.

In his own room he jerked on a pair of running shorts and reached for the small gun safe he kept high on his closet shelf. It had been years since he'd loaded his Glock, but even in the darkness his old speed and efficiency came back to him as if he'd never been away. In seconds he was back out in the hallway and easing toward the open stairway to the main floor.

From downstairs came the sounds of harsh whispers. The sound of glass breaking. A muffled curse. The footsteps were moving faster, now, coming to the bottom of the stairway.

Anger and a surge of protectiveness poured through his veins as he thought of Abby sleeping upstairs, defenseless and unaware. The basset by her bed wouldn't be any more protection than a parakeet if anyone made it up there.

Joe released the safety on his semiautomatic and two-handed it as he moved just far enough to see downstairs. A couple of burly men dressed in black were at the first step. Something silver gleamed in one guy's hands.

"Drop your weapons. *Now,*" Joe announced coldly. "I'm armed and *very* ready to fire."

They froze.

"Now," he barked.

One of them took a step back, stumbled, then pivoted sharply and raced for the front door. The other raised his gun and fired in a blur of motion. Behind Joe, just to the left of his ear, the glass in a picture frame shattered.

Joe took rapid aim and fired back, then ducked behind the corner. From the shadows at the base of the stairs came a low groan.

"Joe! What's going on?" Abby's footsteps flew down the attic staircase behind him.

He motioned her back with one hand, then glanced up at her. *"Quiet."*

Her eyes were huge in her pale face. She stared at his weapon and turned whiter still. *"Guns?* My God!"

"Stay back," he hissed.

Something crashed to the floor downstairs. Footsteps shuffled, and then the front door slammed.

"Wait here." He raced down the stairs to the front door. Outside, a driver peeled out with a squeal of burning rubber.

Damn. In the darkness, he could only see the form of a sedan, but not the make or color.

When he went back inside, Abby met him at the door. "This time I don't care what you say. I'm calling the police. Someone could have been killed here!"

"Wait."

"Are you *crazy?*" Her voice rose in panic. "What's going on? Tell me!" She wrapped her arms around her waist and shivered. "Why do you have a gun, for God's sake? Who were they?"

He turned to lock the front door, then shoved his gun into his back waistband.

He considered and discarded a dozen explanations. But when he saw the fear in her eyes, he knew that only one would do.

The truth.

CHAPTER FIFTEEN

HE KNEW he had to tell the truth. Now he had to decide how much.

Joe paced the kitchen, his frustration rising. So close—he was so close now, yet he could lose all the ground he'd gained if Abby didn't believe him. If she went to Gene, or the cops, or even Louise, the chances of finding a paper trail back to the Ricardo Torres gang would be roughly zero.

Gene was being pressured, and it didn't take much thought to guess who was behind it.

Dressed now, in jeans and a sweater, Abby strode into the kitchen and silently made a pot of coffee, then turned to face him. "Who *are* you?" she demanded. "And what's going on?"

He prayed she would forgive his careful adjustment of the truth when this was all over. The thought of never seeing her again—the thought of her hating him or worse, fearing him—already felt like a knife twisting in his gut. "I...I'm with the DEA."

"You're *what?*" Her mouth dropped open and

she stared at him as a host of emotions showed in her eyes. Disbelief. Assessment. Then betrayal and humiliation, followed by anger so raw and pure that it crackled through the space between them.

"I've been working undercover."

"Either you're lying to me now, or you've been lying to me since the day you first walked in my door. What else about you isn't true? The sad story about your wife? Why Megan is with you?" She gave a bitter laugh. "One heck of a cover. Is Megan even your daughter?"

He steeled himself against her fury. "Of course she is."

"You *used* me." Her hand flew to her throat. "My God, you even slept with me. Was that all a lie, too? To secure your position here? To make sure you seemed credible?"

"God, no, Abby."

She shot him a look of disbelief. "Right. What is that called…collateral damage? All for a good cause?"

"Abby—"

"How do I know you're even telling the truth about being with the DEA?" She narrowed her eyes at him. "Maybe those were the *good* guys who broke in here, and I'm harboring a fugitive."

"Think about it, and tell me you can honestly believe that."

"Then where's your badge? Do you have ID?" She slammed her hands on her hips, waiting. "No? Well, maybe we can call the local DEA office—there ought to be one in this region somewhere. They would verify who you are, right?"

"The locals don't even know I'm here. There's… possible corruption."

She laughed aloud at that. "Silver Springs—a hotbed of crime. What do we have here—a half-dozen deputies? I'm sure it would be easy for a bad one to blend in. 'Hey, Doug—like my new Porsche? My wife saves grocery coupons.'"

"It's not that simple."

The coffeemaker hissed and spat. She turned around and grabbed a couple of mugs from the cupboard, but then just stood there, with her head bowed and hands braced wide on the counter.

He crossed the room and stood behind her, wanting to pull her into her arms, wanting to make everything right. "I never would have slept with you if I didn't truly care, Abby. These past couple of months have been the best of my life, because of you."

"What you're saying," she said coldly, "is that you still need a place to stay." She turned around to face him. "Look, I'm scared. I don't want any part of this—or you."

The emptiness in his heart grew. "I understand."

"What about the police?"

He hesitated. "Report this if you want to, but the cops won't be much help. I didn't get a good look at the suspects' faces, and they were both wearing gloves, so there won't be any prints. I can't ID the make of the car or its plates."

"How convenient, because you don't want the police involved anyhow." She paced to the end of the kitchen and then back again. "You've put us all at risk. How could you do that?"

"You're missing the point, here. The risk was present all along, Abby, simmering just beneath the surface. I'm here to *deal* with it. I only need a little more time, and this will be over. A few days at the most." Joe looked down into her angry face and sighed. "For what it's worth, I'm truly sorry. I never meant to hurt you."

"And I regret the day you walked in my door."

"You want us to leave?"

She took a shaky breath. "For Megan's sake, you can stay…for now. But if anything else happens, you'll be out of here the same day, and I'll call the police to recommend that Megan be placed in protective custody with Social Services until she can be taken back to her aunt and uncle. Is that clear?"

"Totally." He hesitated, then added gently, "But think about what happened. My car was vandalized. Did they know it was mine, or think it was yours? Then two men broke in here...probably related incidents, but we don't know who they were or what they were after. I need to get to the bottom of this before someone gets hurt."

Cheerful voices wafted into the kitchen from the driveway, and a moment later Catherine appeared at the back door with Fred leaning heavily on her arm.

"We made it," she said brightly. "It's great to be home."

ON SUNDAY AFTERNOON, Megan leaned into the corner of Abby's front porch and drew her knees tight to her chest, remembering.

She hadn't had the nightmare in weeks. But last night at Lindsey's, it had come back more terrible than ever before.

She'd awakened with a jerk, smelling once again the spilled gasoline, the hot asphalt and the awful scent of blood.

It had been so real that she'd almost been afraid to look at her arms, expecting to see them covered with blood. But with Sue snoring in the other room and Lindsey snuggled deep in her sleeping bag, there was no one to go to...no one who would really care.

So she'd just curled up in a ball, trying to forget the accident. It had been over three years now, and without looking at pictures she could barely even remember what her mother looked like anymore. How awful was that?

The front door opened and Abby stepped outside. "Hey, I've been looking for you," she said with a smile. "Want to help me in the kitchen?"

Megan shook her head, then rested her chin on her upraised knees and glumly watched an ant crawl up her calf.

"No?" Abby crossed the porch and dropped into one of the white wicker chairs. "I thought you might like to help me decorate a cake."

A brief memory flashed through Megan's mind. She'd been four or five, maybe, and she'd stood on a chair next to Mom while they'd decorated a birthday cake in a rainbow of colors, with squiggles everywhere. As always, the memory left a heavy weight in her chest, and she'd never wanted to help with cakes at Aunt Bonnie's for that reason.

"It's to celebrate Fred coming back to us. I've got five or six different colors of frosting made up, and you can choose the decorator tips—do anything you want. Sound like fun?"

Megan gave a grudging nod, because even

though Abby was smiling, her eyes were sad. And if there was anything Megan knew about, it was sadness. "I guess."

In the kitchen, Abby whipped out a big white apron with a flourish and tied it around Megan's waist, then made her wash her hands. "This is three layers—chocolate-and-white checkerboard inside, because I used a special pan. I figure the white frosting would be a good base for your art-work. What do you think?"

Megan nodded again.

"Hey, is something wrong?" Abby gently lifted Megan's chin with a finger and looked into her eyes. "Were you up too late last night?"

"No."

Abby rested the back of her hand against Megan's forehead. "Do you feel okay?"

A lump formed in her throat and she looked away.

"Hey, honey. Come here." Abby slipped into a kitchen chair and pulled Megan over onto her lap. "I know you're a little big for laps, but I don't think we ever get too big for a hug. What do you think?"

She felt tired, and worried, and suddenly it was too much to hold back. She sniffled as a hot tear trailed down her cheek, then she turned into

Abby's welcoming arms and buried her face against her shoulder.

"Oh, sweetheart," Abby murmured, hugging her tight.

She rocked a little, murmuring soft words and rubbing Megan's back. But instead of helping, it made Megan sob and she cried until she had no tears left. But still Abby held her, and being held felt so good that Megan wished it would never end.

When she finally pulled away, she looked up and saw Abby's eyes were filled with tears, too.

"I'm sorry," Megan whispered, suddenly embarrassed.

"No, no," Abby said quickly. "I can't help it—when someone cries I usually end up crying right along with them. My mom used to say I had a heart of marshmallow."

"My mom—" The memory came back, sweet and gentle, and felt like a burst of sunshine. "My mom said I always had the heart of a woodland sprite because I laughed so much. But after she died…I guess it just went away."

"Things got pretty sad, then."

"Awful." She straightened and plopped onto the chair next to Abby. "I mean, Uncle Carl and Aunt Bonnie were great, but…"

"But no one could replace your mom, right?"

"Sometimes I—" She broke off and looked away.

"What?"

"Sometimes I have really bad dreams." She swallowed hard.

"About the accident?"

Megan nodded.

"I understand you were the only survivor. Anyone would have a tough time with that, especially since this was your mom and stepfather. In fact, there's even a name for it—'survivor's guilt.' A person feels bad because they are so thankful to be alive, yet their loved ones died, so it isn't fair."

"I used to wish that I'd died instead of her, because it hurts so much to lose her. More than anything, I wanted my mom back."

Abby reached out and took Megan's hands in hers. "I think you're a very strong, brave girl, Megan. It takes a lot of time to get over something like this."

"I thought maybe I'd get to stay with my dad, but he doesn't really want me."

"Maybe you could talk to him and tell him how you feel."

"He thinks I'm better off with Aunt Bonnie, 'cause he isn't married and I wouldn't have a mom. That's probably why he let me get Buffy," Megan added glumly. "So he can dump me off at

Aunt Bonnie's house and not feel guilty about leaving me behind.''

"Oh dear," Abby exclaimed. "I don't think that's true at all. Even if he knows he can't take you with him, he loves you, Megan."

"A good dad sticks around. My dad never even visited—not once—in five years."

"Maybe he had a reason?"

"My aunt said it wasn't true, but my cousin teased me a lot. He told me Dad was in *prison*."

Abby frowned. "Kids are mean sometimes, honey. They'll say very cruel things."

Feeling like a traitor for telling, Megan shifted uncomfortably.

The memory of her oldest cousin's taunts still stung. She'd always told him he was lying. He'd even shown her a newspaper clipping once, that he'd found in Uncle Carl's desk, but she'd laughed it off because Dad's last name was common and that article could have been about anyone.

But now...she'd seen Dad slip out sometimes when he thought she was asleep, and it wasn't so hard to imagine that he was doing something he shouldn't. And now that she was older, things were starting to fall into place.

"Megan?" Abby was searching her face now, her eyes wide with concern. "Do you think your cousin was right?"

It was wrong to lie, and it seemed wrong to tell the truth. But maybe if Abby talked to him, she could keep him from what he was doing, and help keep him safe.

And someday, maybe he'd even want to have a real house and family, and might want Megan back.

She looked away, unable to look Abby in the eye. "I saw it in the newspaper."

THE MOMENT ABBY WALKED into the garage, Joe knew he was in trouble. He looked up from the lawn mower he was fueling, straightened, and capped the gas can. "Problems?"

"I wanted to believe you. Dammit, I *cared* about you."

"What's this about, Abby?" He reached for a rag on the workbench and wiped off his hands.

"Just a small matter to you—the truth."

"I don't know what you mean."

"Give me a break. Where did you do time?" Her voice dropped ten degrees.

"Maybe you're not even *supposed* to be out."

"I was released April 9," he said slowly, giving in to the inevitable. "I didn't escape."

"Why come here? Did I look like easy prey? Someone too gullible to be real, maybe? Imagine—believing you were with the DEA."

"I was." He knew everything he'd had, or hoped to have with her in the future, was long gone. The pain of that loss cut deep. "I had to be here because of your husband, Oren."

"*Oren?* He died a year ago." She threw her hands up in disgust.

"Look, I want you to pack your things and—"

"Wait. What do you know about your husband's death?"

"That he died of a heart attack. Everyone knows that."

"It was probably a little more complicated, Abby. Think back, about his habits. His... pleasures." He watched her body language for any hint that she knew, but she just gave him an irritated frown.

"He belonged to the civic organizations in town," she retorted. "He golfed."

"He also had a crack habit that was running around two hundred bucks a day. God only knows how much he was using by the time he died."

She slashed the air in front of her with a hand. "I don't know who you are anymore, and I don't care. You're crazy, and I want you *gone*."

"I *was* DEA then, Abby. I spent almost a year on an investigation of a drug operation, and I was pretty sure your husband was used to launder part of its money. When I got too close, someone planted a few kilos of meth in my car. I spent five years in prison for something I didn't do, and was released on a technicality. That didn't clear my name, so now I need to find out who was behind it all. I want my life back.''

"I…'' Her eyes filled with confusion and disbelief, then she shook her head. "You're wrong. Oren was the most straitlaced person you could ever meet. He never would have fallen into anything like that. We had an excellent income from a good, solid business.''

"Enough,'' Joe said gently, "to support a habit costing hundreds of dollars a day? We set up an undercover dealer, and he bought from her. We had it on film, Abby. And as far as being weak— a lot of users are hooked after just one try, and the addiction is incredibly powerful.''

"This can't be true.'' But now her gaze wavered, and she was biting her lower lip.

"He was in an emotionally stressful profession,'' Joe continued. "Maybe he thought he needed the escape—then couldn't stop. What if he was lured into this, then caught in a web of lies, huge costs and driving needs? And then his supplier says, 'Hey, you work with us a little. We'll cut you a deal on your dope—and you can even get rich with a little operation on the side. What's the harm?'''

"That's ridiculous."

"Then consider this—he was in good health, and he was just middle-aged. How likely is it that he had a sudden heart attack from natural causes? My bet is that he died of cardiac arrest after an especially pure pipeful of his little secret."

"You're a real jerk, you know that?" She gave an impatient wave of her hand. "It's easy to build some incredible story about him now that he isn't here to defend himself. But he's dead now, and it's over."

Joe took a deep breath. "Not exactly. Until I got here, I suspected that you could have been involved."

"You are *crazy,*" she snapped.

"That's why I couldn't explain why I was here. Now I'm pretty sure that your brother-in-law has continued the family tradition."

Her mouth fell open. "*Gene?* He's a prissy, particular guy, and he'd never have anything to do with some lowlife drug dealer. He'd be absolutely appalled at the thought."

"Unless he was strong-armed into it. After that, maybe he found it was pretty easy money. And the thing is…I believe this all leads to the man I was after five years ago. I think he's still involved, and I think he knows that his little operation is at risk.

Which is why my car was vandalized, and why someone was in your house last night."

"Then you've got to leave *now*. I've got Fred and Catherine here—what if something happens to them? And what about your little girl?"

"You said once that Gene refused to let you help with the books. He doesn't trust you, Abby. If he's starting to feel edgy, the suspicion could fall on you, as well. For all we know, those intruders were sent as a warning for you...perhaps they even thought my SUV was one of your vehicles. They might not have seen the out-of-state license plates in the dark."

She wobbled, as if her knees were weak. "Then...I need to call the police."

"I believe the Ricardo Torres gang is behind this. If the police start asking questions, Gene will probably alert his contact and start shredding evidence. Everything I need could disappear. And then what happens? These guys just settle in someplace else, continuing their drug shipments and money laundering. And maybe...just maybe... they'll be a little perturbed over the bother. How safe will you be?"

"So there's no way out."

"I've been biding my time, making careful progress. But what happened last night tells me that time is running out. Since you're a part owner, you have a right to access anything there. If I can establish the paper trail—document any money-laundering activities—we could turn that information over and ultimately take out the entire organization.''

''You want me to walk in there and start going through files? Gene—''

''Not you, just me. Tonight. Tell me where to look.''

She shot an incredulous glance at him. ''You're kidding.''

''Gene hasn't wanted you working on the books, Abby. What will happen if you waltz in there tomorrow and demand the right to search through his records? He could divert you from the key records, hide or destroy the most incriminating documents...or call on his 'friends' for help.''

''Assuming that he has ever done anything wrong.''

''It's more than an assumption. The sooner this is over, the safer you'll be. And,'' he added heavily, ''the sooner I'll be out of your life.''

It took her so long to answer, that he figured she was simply going to walk back to the house and call the cops.

''Okay,'' she said finally. ''I don't know what to believe—God knows *your* track record in hon-

esty is poor. I'll help, but I'm going with you tonight because I need to know the truth. My name
is associated with the Sheltering Pines, after all.
And after this, I want you out of my house.''

CHAPTER SIXTEEN

AFTER ASKING CATHERINE and Fred to watch Megan while she and Joe went out on a "date," Abby endured their delight and gentle teasing for the rest of the evening, and was almost relieved when it was time to leave at eight o'clock. *"To make it sound like a real date,"* Joe had suggested.

As if any woman with a stark-white complexion and shaking hands could possibly be going on a date.

"A *movie?* You want to go to a movie, and just sit there like nothing unusual is going to happen?" Abby stared at Joe from the passenger side of her red Chevy as he pulled out of her driveway and headed toward Main. "That's sort of a stretch, isn't it?"

He shrugged. "It's something to kill time. We should hit the Sheltering Pines at around midnight. Would you rather get something to eat?"

"I'd rather go home and forget any of this ever happened." She bit her lip.

"What do we say if Gene turns up at the funeral home? Or even Louise?"

"We were on a date, and since you've been looking for a copy of your house-insurance policy all day, I said we could stop in so you could check for it in the files."

"That's pretty lame, Coughlin."

"Well, Louise is an employee, so it's none of her business. She has no reason to be there at night, anyway. And Gene—well, what's the worst he can do?"

"Good point. Unless he really does have contacts with all these bad guys you've been talking about—not that I believe it—in which case we could be in a lot of serious trouble."

"Which is why I'd rather have you stay away."

"And why I told you, I had to come along. Just to prove you wrong."

Joe glowered at her. "I could still take you home."

"No."

"At the first sign of trouble, we'll call in the police."

"I thought you said you didn't know who to trust."

"I don't, but if the situation goes south, then the important thing is to keep you safe. I was investigating the Dalton branch of the Sheltering Pines when the county deputies found meth in my car. They testified against me—but did they plant it? I don't know. If one of them did, then he'd been paid off—and there could be the same setup here. Someone on the take, watching out for the local 'business.'"

Abby considered the local deputies. Most of them were young, underpaid, with high-risk jobs and families to feed. What would it take to buy off someone who was barely making ends meet?

Joe pulled to a stop in front of the Ranchman, a dark, rustic steak house that drew the boots-and-jeans crowd almost every night of the week. "Is this okay?"

"Sure—though I don't think I can eat a thing. My stomach is already doing a two-step."

Joe shifted in his seat to face her and draped one wrist over the steering wheel. "Tell me about Louise."

For just a moment, she'd been watching him drive, and imagining this was a real date. Despite everything she knew about him now, Joe Coughlin still had more sheer masculine appeal than anyone she'd ever seen.

That sexy sideways glance when he talked to her as he drove—the ripple of muscle beneath his black polo shirt—even the scent of his aftershave fascinated her. Memories of his kisses—and the times she'd kissed him—still had the power to heat her blood and make her insides jitter.

"Louise?" he repeated, raising an eyebrow.

"Yes…um…" Abby collected her scattered thoughts. "She's a longtime employee. She actually worked at the home in Winthrop with Oren for the last three or four years before he died. Then she came here because she wanted to be closer to her sister."

"What kind of employee files are kept, do you know? References, background checks, and so on?"

She had to smile at that. "These are small towns, in these parts. You stop anyone on the street and they can tell you who your cousins and great-aunts are, who you graduated with in high school, and every embarrassing thing you ever did."

"There aren't any records?"

She tipped her head. "When I worked in the Winthrop office, we had the files for all of the four homes—basic stuff like hire, fire and retirement dates. Family-contact information, the original job application. We really never had many employees, and most are pretty much lifelong."

"I'm mostly just interested in Louise."

"She would wish," Abby said dryly. "She seems to think you're quite a hottie."

"A what?"

"Guess you missed out on that one while you were…away. She thinks you are 'hot stuff.'"

"Is she married?"

"Briefly, years back. Now it's just her and her little dog Twinkles. She's quite the motherly sort, though…she seems concerned about Gene's welfare and was a very efficient gal when she worked for Oren." Abby paused for a moment, considered her neighbor. "I feel sorry for her, a little. Her only sister is fighting cancer and there's no one else in her family who lives around here. I think she's dedicated to her job because she's lonely."

"So she's a model employee, then. What about the employees at the other funeral homes?"

"The newest hire is maybe eight years. Good solid people, all of them. Oren always said his job as overall business manager was made easier by the great employees he had." Abby gave him a narrowed look. "You see? Your suspicions are unfounded. Maybe those things happen in big cities, but not in towns like this one."

He gave her a faint smile as he pulled the keys from the ignition. "I wish you were right. Unfortunately, a lot of drug crime filters out into the rural areas where there's less law enforcement coverage."

Inside the steak house, amid a raucous hubbub of conversations, laughter and the clinking of beer bottles, they found a booth far away from the local country band playing by the crowded dance floor.

After ordering the house special—half-pound ground-sirloin hamburgers crowned with bacon strips and cheddar—Joe nodded toward the dance floor.

"Care to dance?"

"No." She nearly had to shout to be heard over the noise.

His fingers were drumming in time to the throbbing beat of the bass. "Might be fun…I don't remember when I last got to dance." He raised an eyebrow as he leaned closer to her. "It might even make this look like a *real* date."

She wouldn't have accepted, but then he stood and held out a hand, his eyes sparkling with anticipation, and the two cowboys at the next table started whooping and hollering, saying, "Go on, little girl, don't break his heart!"

When she stepped into his arms on the dance floor, the band started a rockin' fifties dance song, and Joe swung her through it with grace and balance until she was dizzy and laughing.

The fast songs took her breath away. And when Joe pulled her tighter against the hard wall of his chest, the slow ones threatened her heart.

After they'd eaten, he took her out to the dance floor once more, and while swaying to "Unchained

Melody,'' he leaned closer. ''I've missed this,'' he murmured next to her ear. ''What about you?''

''It's been a long time.'' Probably since her teenage dating years, though it sounded too pathetic to admit. And she'd never danced with anyone as smooth as Joe.

He glanced at his watch. ''Time to go.''

Startled, she lifted her own wrist to check the time. She'd expected long and awkward silences interspersed with game efforts at conversation—an interminable several hours. Instead, he'd made her laugh and feel eighteen again, and the evening had flown by.

Out in the Chevy, he studied her for a moment before turning his attention to the ignition. ''Thank you,'' he said, his gaze on the rearview mirror as he backed out of the parking space. ''You did well. Anyone watching would have thought we were a couple.''

She'd drifted all too easily into the magic of the evening, enjoying his conversation, savoring his touch. Just a quick, sideways slide of his silvery gaze had the power to send shivers clear to her toes, and make her think of long dark nights and cool satin sheets.

But of course, none of it was real…and she'd been a fool to think otherwise. ''Now what?''

''We're still on this date, so we can't park at

your house. Fred might wander out to chitchat the time away. I was thinking we might park a block or two down and walk back.''

Ten minutes later the vehicle was parked over on Hawthorne, and Joe and Abby were hovering at the back door of the funeral home. Abby tried one key and then another from the heavy ring Oren had left in his top dresser drawer.

''I think Gene changed the locks,'' she muttered, trying the last key. ''This is taking forever.''

The last key jammed.

Joe reached over Abby's shoulder and closed his hand over hers, then gave the key a swift jiggle. The door swung wide and they both slipped in, shutting the door behind them.

Abby shuddered.

''Are you okay?'' Joe moved to the electrical panel on the wall and disabled the security system using the code Abby gave him.

''Y-yes—it's just so dark and gloomy. And I still think this is a crazy idea.''

''Let's get done then, so we can get out of here.'' He lifted his chin toward the staircase leading to the second floor. ''From what I've been able to see, there are two tiers of file drawers plus a stack of storage boxes in the spare room up there, and several four-drawer cabinets in Gene's office.

In the basement, there's at least one storage room that he seems concerned about.''

"Let's start at the top—the most current records ought to be up there. You're sure he's gone tonight?''

Joe nodded. "I cruised by his house just before we left tonight, and he was outside on his front porch with a tall glass of something, reading the newspaper. He didn't look like he was going anywhere.''

GENE STROKED Godiva's rabbit-soft fur, then put the cat down on her favorite velvet chair by the front window and started upstairs. He winced as he stepped wrong on his left foot—a reminder of the night several weeks ago when Tom Baker had turned up in his office.

He'd been sure Tom was going to kill him right then and there. The man was big and powerful and evil, and Gene still had the bruises to show for it— bruises that even Beige 4 Discoloration Mask didn't conceal completely.

Before he'd left, Tom had bared his teeth in a semblance of a smile. "The only reason you're alive is because the boss figures you're still useful.'' He spat on the floor. "The next time you screw up, you'd better start running, because we ain't taking no more chances with you. The next time, you die.''

After that night, Gene had slept at the funeral home for over a week, afraid to leave anything to chance.

But now…he smiled as he surveyed his home from the top step of his open staircase, admiring the new burgundy leather sofa and chairs showcased against the off-white carpeting. Surely he could just kick back and enjoy what he'd earned over the past year. The white lacquer grand piano. The nice Jacuzzi in the bathroom, where he was headed right now.

He already had his heavy velour robe off and was leaning over to check his bathwater, when an air current fluttered a piece of paper stuck to the mirror over the vanity.

Strange—his cleaning lady, Marie, always left messages on the kitchen table. He would certainly need to have a word with her when he saw her next. Certain procedures were required in this house, and he enforced each one to the letter.

Frowning, he reached over and grabbed the note.

YOU'VE BEEN WARNED…AND NOW YOU'RE DEAD.

Panic slammed through him, raising goose bumps on his flesh and pitching his stomach into an angry sea. *Someone had been in his house.* In his bathroom. Walking on his beautiful white carpet. Maybe going through his things.

Maybe they were even still here.

With shaking hands he grabbed his robe and put it on, knotting the belt tight. Scrambled through his options.

The phone in his bedroom.

The phone downstairs.

The cell phone still in his sport-coat pocket, hanging neatly in the front closet.

All three meant leaving the locked safety of his bathroom and stepping out into the unknown…and all three meant that the cops would come. There would be questions.

A sob rose in his throat as he fastened his trembling, sweaty fingers on the doorknob…then let his hand fall to his side.

His heart beating wildly, he flipped off the bathroom exhaust fan and leaned his bulk against the door, listening. Five minutes. Six. Seven.

After fifteen minutes he cracked the door open. Hesitated. Then opened it wider. A fresh breeze wafted into the steamy bathroom—very odd, because he always kept the windows closed and doors locked, preferring filtered air to anything coming in from outdoors.

Gathering his faltering courage, he made his way slowly across the open balcony, darting glances around him every step of the way. The heavy silence told him no one was here, yet fear clogged his throat as he made his way down the steps.

The blue-velvet chair was empty.

"Godiva?" he whispered. "Kitty-kitty-kitty?"

She always came on ballerina-light feet, her plume of a tail raised. But the house was still and silent as a funeral vault.

At the base of the steps he gripped the railing and stared.

The front door was wide open.

Waves of hot and cold swamped his senses, and bright lights sparked at the edge of his vision. Reeling, he gripped the stair railing with both hands.

It had been so easy, juggling the books for the four funeral homes…finding ways to slip in a few thousand here, few thousand there. In a cash-based business dealing in flowers, high-ticket items and people immersed in grief, there were lots of ways.

Now that snare of easy money and false security tightened like a noose around his neck.

In the back of his mind he'd always known the day could come when he might have to disappear.

One didn't deal with the scum of the earth and expect a comfortable retirement.

He'd pack his bags, then collect the most crucial documents at the Sheltering Pines…in case he needed them later to bargain for his life.

"ALL I'M FINDING are product catalogs, old correspondence and funeral contracts," Abby announced, cutting an anxious glance at the digital clock on Gene's desk. "It all looks normal to me."

"Keep looking." Joe lifted another box off a closet shelf and set it on the floor. "There should be invoices and deposits that don't match. Unusually large statements from companies that have the same—or similar—addresses. Large amounts that have been written off, say, for wilted flowers or shipping damage. Altered figures on statements."

"I'd be first in line to agree Gene isn't a pleasant guy, but I just can't see him ever having the street smarts to handle anything that complex…or risky."

In the dim glow of his flashlight, Joe's dark features were resolute as he folded the flaps of the box down and set it aside. "You'd be surprised."

"Look, we've been through that storeroom up here, Louise's office, and now Gene's. I'll give this another ten minutes and then I'm going home." She pulled out another file drawer and thumbed through the folder tabs. "I think I've been more than fair about this."

"We still have the basement."

She gave a sound of exasperation. "There's nothing down there—other than the embalming rooms, cold storage, chemicals and records that go back twenty years or more. None of that would be of any use."

His faint smile sent a chill down her back. "I wouldn't be so sure."

"I hope you—"

Joe abruptly raised a hand and froze.

"I don't hear—"

"*Quiet.*"

Abby closed her eyes and listened. Outside, leaves rustled in a fitful breeze. A distant owl gave a plaintive cry.

And a floorboard creaked downstairs.

Her eyes flew open wide. "Is that Gene?"

Joe cocked his head and listened. "I'd guess it is, but I don't think he's coming up here. Hear that?"

She closed her eyes and concentrated.

"The elevator is going down to the basement—can you hear it now?"

"No, but I'm glad. Let's get out of here!"

"Not yet. Gene might just do us a favor." He rose easily to his feet and helped her up, then grabbed the boxes on the floor and put them back in the closet. After a quick survey of the room, he started for the door. "I'll bet he can find what we need faster than we can."

"You're going down there?" Nervous tingles raced down Abby's spine.

"I wasn't expecting company, but if I don't miss my guess, this might be 'now or never.'" He paused at the door. "I think you'd better go home."

"Not on your life. My reputation is at stake here, too."

"Then just stay way back and out of sight, understand? When you corner a dog, even a gentle one might turn vicious because it's scared. With Gene...I just don't know."

Good analogy. Abby gave a vague wave of her hand, promising nothing, and followed Joe as he eased down the stairs. At the basement landing he opened the door inch by inch, his body tense.

The broad, white-tiled hall was empty beneath the stark glow of the overhead lights. Halfway down, one of the doors leading into the embalming room was ajar and light spilled out into the hall.

"Now, you stay here—by the stairs. If you hear anything, I want you to *move*. Get out of here fast, and don't take any chances. When you're safe, use your cell phone and call for help."

She'd been angry at his deception. Hurt. But now she felt a flash of concern. "Maybe this isn't such a good idea. We can come back tomorrow during the day and just demand some answers.

"Nice thought, but I don't think Gene will be here to answer them." He turned and looked her in the eye, then suddenly looped an arm around her shoulders and drew her into a swift, hard kiss. "When this is over, you and I need to talk."

It wasn't hard to guess what he would say. "Thanks for the help...have a nice life." Then he'd ride off into the sunset. A man like him didn't settle down in places like Silver Springs.

She'd make sure he never knew how much she really cared.

CHAPTER SEVENTEEN

MOTIONING FOR ABBY to stay put, Joe moved slowly, silently down the hall.

He should have come alone.

But she'd insisted, and he'd rationalized to himself that her knowledge of the filing and book-keeping systems might give them an advantage. He'd been right on that score, but he hadn't expected Gene to show up.

At the edge of the open doorway he eased forward until he could peer inside.

The air was cool, slightly damp, and pungent with the odors of disinfectants and chemicals he couldn't identify. A rush of cool air flowed into the room—probably due to a specialized exhaust system.

Clean white tiling covered the floor and walls. On wire-mesh shelving were gallon jugs of chemicals, row upon row of smaller bottles of solvents, arterial embalming fluids and cosmetics, and clear plastic boxes filled with odd assortments of plastic devices. A traffic jam of gleaming metal equipment carts filled one corner of the room, while red plastic biohazard bags hung from metal frames by the pair of stainless-steel tables in the center of the room.

Slipping the Glock from the waistband holster at the small of his back, Joe took another step forward, and then another, his senses on high alert. At the sounds of rustling papers he moved in a little closer.

The room was L-shaped. Now he could see around the bend to a bank of stainless-steel doors set in the wall. One door was open wide, its body tray pulled forward.

There wasn't a body on this one, though. There were boxes, and Gene was scrambling through them with a definite sense of desperation.

"Interesting filing system you have there," Joe said as he moved into the room.

Gene spun around, his face a mask of shock and horror, papers flying out of his hands. "You!"

"Yeah, just me. What are you doing, a little housekeeping after midnight?"

Gene uttered a foul curse as he scrambled to catch the falling documents.

"You have no right to be down here."

"But *I* do, Gene." Abby skirted the tables and moved back into the alcove, drawing close enough to see the stack of papers Gene had already stuffed into the suitcase at his feet. "Is this why you were so careful to keep me away?"

Gene shot a look of loathing at her. "You have no idea what it takes to run this place. But you should know better than to bring anyone down here."

If Joe still had any doubts about Abby's innocence, they would have been laid to rest by the anger flashing in her eyes.

"I didn't believe Joe at first, but I should have," she snapped. "What's going on here?"

Gene shoved more papers into the suitcase, then rose and grabbed another handful from the cardboard box. "It's not my fault, you know. Oren was the one. I didn't even know until he was dead—and then I had no choice. They would have killed me, dammit."

"They? Who are 'they'?" Abby demanded.

Joe motioned for her to back off. "It's over now, Gene. You aren't going anywhere."

Behind them, the doors to the preparation room hit the tiled walls at either side with a crash, revealing two burly men in jeans, ripped T-shirts and studded biker boots. Both aimed AK–47 assault rifles at Joe's heart.

"You aren't going anywhere, either," growled the one with tattoos snaking up his arm. "Get your hands up—or someone gets wasted right now."

From the corner of his eye Joe saw Abby pull back deeper into the alcove, the cell phone in her hand hidden from Gene's line of vision. She hit a single button—speed dial for 911, he hoped—and dropped the phone into her jacket pocket.

Joe turned, keeping his hands low and his gun out of sight. He slid it beneath a stack of plastic sheeting on the table in front of him and raised his hands in one smooth motion. And looked into the face of a man he knew all too well.

The tallest of the two, Aaron had been his key informant during his last case five years ago.

"Get your hands up where I can see them. Now."

"So Ricardo owns you," Joe said grimly. "I wonder who might have set me up. Now I know."

"I went where the money was, man." Aaron's eyes glittered. "Ricardo knew you were getting too close to the action, and he needed you out of the way."

Gene looked wildly between them, then fixed the tattooed guy with a beseeching look. "I had nothing to do with him, Tom. I swear. He's been nosing around, and the girl, too. She's hiding right over here."

Aaron scowled and motioned with the barrel of his rifle, and his companion swung wide enough into the room to take aim at her.

Her face white, she edged into the room.

"We can finally finish this, no?" Aaron's eyes gleamed with satisfaction.

"The boss don't like loose ends."

"No, he doesn't." Louise strolled in the door behind Aaron, her bright peach sweat suit at odds with the hard tone of her voice. "And we're running into a lot of them here."

Abby drew in a sharp breath. *"Louise?"*

The older woman ignored her. "We might as well do them right here…then bake them with all those papers over there, so there's nothing left to find but ashes."

"Wait—Louise!" Gene's voice rose an octave. His face was beaded with sweat. "This is a mistake. Just ask Tom. He'll set this all straight."

"He isn't going to help you—he's been following orders all along." Joe flicked an impatient glance in Gene's direction. "Oren's deal was with the Ricardo Torres gang. If you ever read the newspaper, you have an idea of what you've been dealing with."

"But *Louise.* I thought…"

"I imagine they've been giving Louise a nice cut," Joe said. "Just to keep an eye on things and make sure everything continued to run smoothly."

Abby stared at the older woman. "You were in

this with *Oren?* He and you…'' Dawning compre-
hension played across her features. ''My God.''

''He was planning to divorce you before he
died,'' Louise said with a bitter smile. ''He and I
would have been so very happy…but then he
started doing crack, and slid into a partnership with
Ricardo to help pay the bills. With Oren gone, I
just continued our little business agreement.''

Abby paled. ''His heart attack…''

''The crack, probably. But I never would have
stained his memory by revealing it to anyone
who'd be around long enough to spread the word.''

''But—but—'' Gene's face reddened. ''I did it
all. I handled the books. It was me who made the
contact every month!''

''Oh, please.'' The older woman gave him a
contemptuous glance. ''Someone had to re-check
everything you did. Good God, Gene—you never
did catch on, and the arrangement here was just
too perfect to give up. Everything worked just fine
until Abby's pal showed up.''

''W-we can salvage this deal. I know we can!''

''Right!'' Her mouth curled with disgust. ''Ricardo sent Tom out to scare you a little, and here
you are, making our final job easier by grabbing
all the documents we needed to find. Exactly what
we hoped for.'' She flicked a glance at Aaron and
Tom. ''Boys?''

Joe edged closer to the table in front of him, judging the distance and position of his weapon.

From outside came the sound of wailing sirens.

Abby caught and held his gaze for a split second, then she screamed, full throttle. In the ceramic-tiled room the sound echoed. The gunmen wavered for just a millisecond. Louise ran for the door.

Joe dropped lower, palmed his Glock and squeezed off three rounds from the hip.

The shorter gunman screamed and grabbed his leg. Turning awkwardly, he managed one faltering step, then fell against the wall.

Aaron jerked his rifle higher and pulled the trigger, his aim going wild as he swung the barrel between Joe and Abby.

Joe fired again, this time hitting center mass. Aaron blanched as his knees buckled. Vaulting over the table, Joe grabbed their guns and took off after Louise.

He caught up with her at the stairwell and slammed the door before she could get through it. "Leaving so soon? I was looking forward to having a really long talk with you."

BY THE TIME the police finished their questions and hauled Gene, Louise and the gunmen away, dawn was breaking over the treetops to the east, and Abby had regained some of her color.

"Tough night," Joe said as he took her arm and walked her back to her house.

She'd answered questions by the police, but hadn't so much as glanced in Joe's direction. He could only imagine what this had done to her—even an agent never got used to facing down a direct assault.

"You did darn well," he added into the silence. "Good thinking, when you speed dialed 911."

On the front porch of her house he stopped, gently took her shoulders in his hands and looked into her pale, expressionless face. "I know you're exhausted, and I also know this has been overwhelming. But you were incredible—and because of you, a lot of good things are going to happen."

She flicked a brief glance up at him, then started to turn toward her front door, but he held her back.

"Please...just listen to me. Gene is already singing his heart out to the DEA agents who got here a few minutes ago. With that, and the evidence they can gather, there'll be a whole list of charges against Torres, and this time they're going to stick. Money laundering, racketeering, drug trafficking, intent to commit murder...his whole network is going down."

"Louise and Gene?"

"Money laundering is a federal offense, so they won't be out on the streets for a good long while. And as for me—this will clear my name. I owe you, Abby."

She gave him a weary smile. "Then settle down somewhere and give that daughter of yours what she needs. A father, and a stable home. I wish you all the best."

Joe searched her face for any sign of forgiveness, or any remnant of caring, but she might as well have been a stranger in a crowded street.

He'd won all he'd wished for during every endless minute he'd spent at Coldwater—vindication, his freedom, a chance now to return to his old career or try anything else in the world without a conviction record holding him back.

But now that sense of victory paled in contrast to the empty, aching space in his chest.

"I need to meet with the police and the DEA tomorrow," he said. "After that, there's just a week of school left."

Her head bowed, Abby nodded.

"I...don't want you to feel uncomfortable. Maybe it would be better if Megan and I moved. There's a little bed-and-breakfast close to Sue and Lindsey's new place. We don't have much here, so it wouldn't take long to pack."

Abby flinched, then lifted her chin. "Fine, if that's what you want. No hard feelings."

He'd hoped she would insist they stay. Now he studied the freckles across her nose, her gentle hazel eyes and the deep, gleaming waves of auburn hair that framed her delicate face, memorizing each feature.

He'd been undercover countless times, portraying dopers and dealers and city guys looking for a little thrill. It was like an acting job on the side, and he'd done it well. But the hardest thing he'd ever had to do was at this moment, as he looked down at Abby Hilliard and gave her the offhand smile of a casual acquaintance, knowing he would never see her again.

He took a deep breath. "No hard feelings at all."

CHAPTER EIGHTEEN

SHE SAW JOE ON the sidewalk with Megan and her puppy once or twice during the following week while driving to the store. Megan waved and Joe nodded to her, but both of them seemed so subdued that she hadn't pulled over.

Fred and Catherine were back home and back to bickering—though now in a playful manner—but her big old house felt empty and cold. Even Hamlet seemed depressed over the loss of his little buddy.

Though in a basset, it was hard to tell.

On Wednesday, Rick had pulled his patrol car to a stop outside her house and had come to her door with Gene's cat. Injured—probably in cat fights—but on the mend after six stitches and a start on antibiotics, Godiva had been roaming the streets frightened and bedraggled. She had been finally identified by her rabies tags.

Abby settled into one of the wicker chairs on the porch and began flipping through a stack of travel brochures. Summer school started next week, and in two months she would be ready to graduate, sell out, pack up and move on. But the excitement she'd felt a few months ago had faded, leaving in its wake a pervasive sense of melancholy.

Ridiculous, she reminded herself firmly. A new career and a new life were waiting somewhere on the horizon, offering the challenges and a chance for happiness she'd dreamed of for a long time.

Ironic, really.

Once held here in Silver Springs by her need to finish school and concern for her boarders, she'd been eager to start over in a new town, far away from Gene and the memories of her troubled marriage.

But Gene would stay behind bars for decades and she could choose to stay here…yet now the old house held even deeper, more painful memories.

Of a man she'd come to love deeply.

Of a little girl who'd lost too much, and deserved a loving and stable home.

Their voices would echo in this house, reminding her of what might have been.

At the sound of toenails scrabbling along her sidewalk, she glanced up to find Buffy dragging Megan behind him, his tail wagging furiously and tongue lolling. He cannonballed into Abby's lap, wiggling and licking her cheek.

Megan flopped down next to her. "I'm teaching him to heel," she said somberly. "We're just having a little trouble."

Abby smothered a smile. "Looking good, though. Maybe you can sign him up for obedience lessons."

"Maybe."

"How do you like your new place?" Abby reached out and gave her a quick hug. "I miss you all. I think even Hamlet does, though he hasn't said it in so many words."

"Why did we have to move?"

Oh, dear. Abby considered her words carefully. "I think your dad just needed to be here during his investigation."

"But I *liked* it here. And I really like you."

"And I like you, too. But sometimes, things work out differently than we want."

"Do you like my dad?"

There was such a hopeful gleam in her eyes that Abby gave her another hug.

"Of course I do. He's a very nice man."

"I mean, do you *like* him?"

The waters were turning more treacherous now, so Abby tousled Megan's hair and grinned. "I think there are a lot of women who would just adore having a chance to go out with him. By the way, does he know where you are right now?''

''I said I was walking Buffy around the block, so I'll go right back.'' She bit her lower lip. ''I know I probably shouldn't ask a favor, but will you come to my end-of-the-school-year party? Everyone's mom is bringing cupcakes or cookies and stuff. And, well…''

Abby's heart went out to her. ''Of course I will. I'd be honored.''

''Really?'' From a distance came the sound of Joe calling Megan's name. ''Oops—I'd better go. Thanks a million, Abby! It's at three o'clock on Friday—City Park, by the wading pool.''

ON FRIDAY MORNING Abby baked a big pan of double-fudge brownies. At three o'clock she arrived at the park, then sat on a bench and looked at her watch. The time was right—did she have the wrong day? There was no one else around except for an older couple strolling along the concrete path and several young moms chasing toddlers over by the swing sets.

Kicking off her shoes, she set the foil-covered pan on a park bench. Then she wandered over to the pool to wiggle her toes in the water. She'd once imagined coming to this very pool with toddlers of her own…back in the days when her marriage was new and still held promise. And now…

"This must be the party."

The deep, familiar voice startled her, and she turned to see Joe standing a few yards away with a Myers Bakery sack held in one hand.

"I'm beginning to wonder," she replied. "The attendance seems pretty light so far. Want a brownie?"

His eyes were dark, intense, searching, but his mouth lifted into a grin as he sat down next to her.

"Only if you'd like to trade for a chocolate-chip cookie."

"You don't suppose…"

Joe glanced around the deserted park. "A definite possibility. Megan just hasn't seemed the same since we left your place."

"Children are so innocent, aren't they?" Abby said lightly. "The world is a fair and honest place, and there are happy endings in every story."

"How about for you, Abby? I've thought about you a lot over the past few days."

She reached for his bakery sack and withdrew a cookie. "Gene will need money for his defense, so he's agreed that we should sell off the funeral homes. That's sure my favorite option. I'll have money for a house somewhere else and some to put away for the future. A happy ending? Not really. Oren and I didn't have much of a marriage, but I'm horrified by what he did. I should have seen what was going on.''

"He lied, he kept you away from the business and distanced himself from you just to be safe, but he couldn't have kept that up forever.''

"And Louise—'' Abby shuddered as she searched her memory for clues and still came up blank. "I thought she was a lonely woman who stopped in all the time just to have someone to talk to. Here she was really just keeping tabs on her little business concern. It scares me to realize that I didn't catch on to either of them.''

"They were both very careful, and very motivated.'' He gave a wry smile.

"People associate drug use with the under-twenty crowd, but older people can hide it easier—they have their own homes, more money and no parental supervision.''

Abby cocked her head and studied him, already seeing such a change. The edge of anger and tension was gone. He seemed far more confident and at ease—a man in control of his future.

Already knowing the answer, she asked, "So how about you—happy endings after all?''

He leaned over, resting his forearms on his thighs with his hands clasped, and stared out over the rippling water of the pool. "The DEA has reviewed the records, and has offered me a job—same level of seniority.''

"In California?'' She held her breath, guessing that it would be someplace far away.

"Here. I've also got an opportunity out in Sacramento. An old buddy wants to start up a security firm, and I've always thought I might want to try that. I'd eventually have employees doing the fieldwork and be able to stay at home more.''

"Better for Megan, then—if she's staying with you?''

"She is. She needs me, and I need her more than words can say. We've both had too much time away from a real family.''

"How is she doing with the fact that you were in prison?''

"She'd had suspicions for some time, I guess. It scared her, thinking I'd done something that bad. Now—'' He gave a wry laugh. "She's sort of elevated me to hero status. And now she has visions of a perfect life in family all her own, with white picket fences and a cozy house with pretty flower beds and fresh, warm cookies everyday.''

"Any child's dream, I'm sure.''

He fell silent for a long moment. "The thing is, it probably isn't going to happen.''

"But surely it will!''

He shifted on the bench to face her. "Megan

may have set this meeting up, but I've been thinking about you—about us—since the last time we were together. There's so much that's wrong…'' His voice drifted off as he searched her face. ''The way we met, the undercover lies between us. I know you feel betrayed, and angry, and I don't blame you.''

Time seemed to stand still and the world narrowed to just Joe's deep voice, his lean and handsome face. Her heart lifted with sudden hope and forgiveness.

''There's no one else who has ever made me feel this way. I look at my career options trying to decide what to do, and all I can think is that nothing else matters if both you and Megan can't be there with me. I love you, Abby. Please give me another chance.'' He reached up and stroked her cheek with his thumb, then drifted a sweet, gentle kiss across her mouth. ''I can't imagine going through life without you. Marry me.''

His touch was feather soft, but she felt it all the way to her bones. Anticipation, and joy, and love washed through her at the thought that she could share the future with a man she'd fallen for from almost the instant they met.

She curved her arms around him and kissed him back, melting into the wash of incredible sensations that she'd never felt with anyone but him, knowing that he was everything she could ever want—a wonderful father, strong and honorable and true. A man she would love forever, with all her heart.

"I don't need to give you a second chance, Joe," she whispered. "I already know. The answer is *yes*."

His gaze burned into hers, and then he claimed her mouth once more, promising everything she'd ever hoped for and never thought she would find.

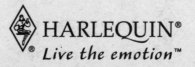

HARLEQUIN *Super* ROMANCE

Nothing Sacred
by Tara Taylor Quinn

Shelter Valley Stories

Welcome back to Shelter Valley, Arizona. This is the kind of town everyone dreams about, the kind of place everyone wants to live. Meet your friends from previous visits—including Martha Moore, divorced mother of teenagers. And meet the new minister, David Cole Marks.

Martha's still burdened by the bitterness of a husband's betrayal. And there are secrets hidden in David's past.

Can they find in each other the shelter they seek? The happiness?

By the author of *Where the Road Ends*, *Born in the Valley* and *For the Children*.

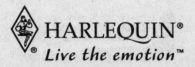

HARLEQUIN®
Live the emotion™

Visit us at www.eHarlequin.com

HSRNSTTQ

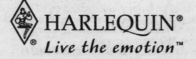

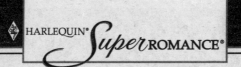

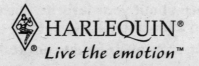

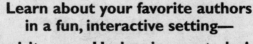

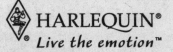